To
Keep
Silent

Thomas Sachs

To
Keep
Silent

Thomas Sachs

ISBN: 978-19159-525-4-7 (hardcover)
ISBN: 978-19159-525-5-4 (perfect bound)
ISBN: 978-19159-525-6-1 (epub)

First printed October, 2025
by Sphinx (an imprint of Sul Books, LTD)
Lewes, UK / Rodenbourg, LUX
Interior and Cover Design: Sul Books

Find our books at SULBOOKS.COM

To RDG, RDG and OMG: my bats in the belfry

To CH, SC, TS, SS and EP: fellow cruisers of the realms

And to Mrs. Puckle, who saw the swamp monsters right away.

ONE

The last of the warmth was venting from his coffee, wisps of steam rising into the car's chilly air like sad ghosts. One of these phantoms turned to him, its mouth stretching open to speak. The weak sun, suddenly reflecting sharp and bright off the silver chrome of tour buses, wrenched this specter from his vision and its message with it. He felt a dull pang of loss, edged with annoyed embarrassment at his attempt to divine a message from the fumes of disgusting gas station coffee.

Autumn wind skittered dry leaves across his long brown car, a few of them finding their way in through the half-lowered window. An open briefcase on the passenger side of the bench seat surrendered loose papers to the gust. Nick lurched to grab them from the air, stuffed them back into the belly of the cracked faux-leather case, and snapped the lid shut.

The buses slowed to a stop in the far corner of the parking lot. Nick rolled the window up and sipped his tepid coffee, then looked from the parking lot to his rearview mirror.

"Nick Kyle, I'm sort of a private private investigator," he said to his reflection.

It didn't sound right, so he tried again. "Nick Kyle, I'm sort of a 'private' private investigator." Still wrong. He smoothed back his black hair, matted it down with licked fingers, showed his smile, took some of the flirt out of the introduction, tried again.

The door of one of the buses opened, and long-haired figures in black descended the steps. Nick watched them pull out cigarettes, hesitate, and then vanish back into the bus. He took another sip of his coffee and waited. The same two men came out again, this time wearing black leather jackets, and then two more men joined them.

Nick's periphery bloomed color: a fat man in a red jacket, thinning hair pulled back in a patchy ponytail, was carrying a large two-way radio and walking towards the bus. The men at the bus tossed their cigarette butts, ground them out with the heels of black boots, and then shook hands with Red Jacket, who spoke into the blocky radio, paused, listened, and then spoke into the radio again. Some kind of business had been settled: the fat man pulled an envelope from an inside jacket pocket, waddled up the bus stairs, stopped halfway, and held the envelope out, then waddled back down the stairs without it. He then motioned for the first two guys to follow him. The three of them crossed the parking lot and disappeared into the building.

Nick had to turn his attention away from the bus to look at the photo on top of the messy stack of papers — a bad, distant profile view of a guy with short hair, hand-dated two years prior.

Nick tried to imagine what two years' hair growth would make the man look like. That amount of time could change an appearance considerably — something he remembered from the time Floriana shaved her head. He'd been surprised by how different she had looked at each stage of its regrowth. One day on the beach, exactly a year before she disappeared, he'd looked over, expecting to find a woman with a short-cropped head; but, instead, he found an expensive bob shining on top of a tanned body in a white bikini. It had taken so long to grow back, but, that day, at that angle, with that sunlight, she was suddenly there. Radiant Flor. Still beautiful every minute of it, he thought. Ominously beautiful, one of those looks that was ... spiritual. She would have laughed at that word and chided him for using it.

Nick wiped away the fog of his breath accumulating on the cold windshield and stared harder at the bus doors as if he could will this man — Brock, or Brocken the file said — to walk through them.

On cue, the doors opened and a load of people stumbled out, every one of them with the same long hair and matching black leather jackets. Nick held up the photo and felt his despair rise. There was no telling them apart, and he laughed in frustration, noting the irony of the uniform in a subculture that allegedly shunned conformity.

He took one last sip of his coffee and pulled the key from the ignition. The door creaked open, and his feet touched down before his eyes saw the puddle. He'd tucked his blue jeans into the vintage Tony Lamas that Flor had bought for him, and the splash of water soaked the exposed pant legs. He felt the water drip down, saturating the socks and pooling in the cup of the heel.

He shut the car door too hard and began walking towards the buses, trying to ignore the squelching footfalls that he knew were only getting louder with each step. When he figured he was close enough, he put on the look he'd been practicing in his rear-view mirror.

They were all staring straight at him. He didn't recognize Brock in the group, but he remembered the way he felt when the cops who'd been asking him questions about the disappearance had crossed their arms, so he crossed his arms in mimicry, hoping he looked tough.

"I'm looking for Brock."

The men kept smoking and staring at him.

"Uh, Brocken, um —" He'd left the file in the car, had no last name. "Brocken, Brock," he said again.

"Show's not for another couple hours," said a voice behind Nick. He turned and saw a man — button up shirt and a little older than everyone else — glancing at his watch. "Can we help you with something?"

"I'm not looking for an autograph, I'm looking for Brock," Nick said again, hoping the switch to a shorter name signaled some kind of intimacy.

"And why are you looking for him unless you want an autograph?"

"I have some, uh—" Nick said, coughing from the smoke that had blown towards him. "I'm Nick Kyle, I'm a—" he stopped, then the words came to him, hand-delivered by a messenger angel. "I'm a secret private investigator." He knew how stupid it sounded the moment he said it, hearing the laughter, but he didn't break eye contact.

"John Skull, tour manager. What's a secret private investigator?"

"'Skull' your real name?" Nick said, trying to keep his voice deep.

"Sculia. What can we help you with, secret private investigator Nick?"

More laughs erupted behind him.

"Brock," Nick said, hoping John would fill in the last name voluntarily. John didn't. "I have some information for him. And I'd like some information from him."

"What kind of information?" John said, then turned. "Brian, start loading the drums in." The bald, shiny head of the one called Brian shuffled away to a trailer hooked to the back of the bus. "Hey Nick Kyle, hate to interrupt you here, but we have a show to set up."

"It really is very important that I talk to Brock." The desperation in Nick's voice checked John, who involuntarily made eye contact with another unremarkable metal-head leaning against the bus.

"If you're a cop, let's see your badge," John said.

"Not a cop, no badge."

"Let's see an ID, then."

"I left it in the car."

"Well, that's unfortunate. You won't be allowed into the venue to watch the show without ID."

"I don't want to see the show. Just Brock."

"Well, if you buy a ticket to the show, you can see him. They're playing tonight. 7PM doors. Oh, look," John said, pointing. A guy on a ladder was adding letters to the marquee, announcing the show as sold out. "Cool for us, sucks for you, man. Maybe you can come to the Milwaukee show. We have to start loading in now, nice to meet you, Nick Kyle."

"I have information about Horace," Nick said to stony silence.

"We can call security if we need to, man," John said, his voice a frequency lower in friendliness.

"I have information about Floriana Gonzalez-Sanchez," Nick said, hoping to catch someone react to the name. The guy against the bus was looking at the ground, smoking, the cherry at the end of the cigarette refracting off a gold ring snug around his middle finger. Nick unconsciously turned towards him, and John caught the subtle movement.

"Okay, man," John said, twisting a knob. The radio came to life with a beep and squawked. "The hard way."

The orange and yellow sparks of the discarded cigarette jumped off the asphalt. "It's cool, John, just give us a minute."

Two

The inside of the bus was cleaner than Nick thought it would be. He declined a beer but accepted some coffee. When the mug was placed in front of him, he wrapped his hands around it, feeling them warm up and trying to avoid looking at the shapes of the vapor. He consciously hunched his body to appear smaller, hoping that less-daunting body language would provoke Brock to open up.

"You prefer Brock or Brocken?" Nick asked, then sipped from the mug.

"Brock. Ericsson," Brock said, filling in the blank. "Are you a cop?"

"I'm definitely not a cop," Nick said with a small laugh, the coffee raising his temperature and his confidence.

"You're not a private investigator either, are you?"

"Like I said, I'm a private private investigator. You can't walk down the street and into my office." Nick liked how that sounded.

Brock turned to look out the window. "That's not what you said before."

Shit, Nick thought, *have I lost him already?* Clueless which question to ask next, he took another sip of warm coffee and hoped the way would open before him.

The flurry of activity outside the window indicated to Brock that everything had started — load-in on their third headlining US tour, crowds big enough now to pay for buses. Not bad for a death metal band. And then this guy had shown up and said *her* name.

All at once, the incident with Flor four years ago was in front of him; the way it had felt when it started, the way everything unfolded like it had its own will, the cycle of it, how everyone knew their role and stepped into it, the professionalism of a tight-knit capable crew: simple steps and actions unfolding into cosmic complexity. To his surprise, the feeling in his stomach as Jared's car had approached the ritual site was nearly identical to the lead-up to showtime.

Brock remembered the way he had looked back to the copse of trees, into that darkness, expecting to see a raging inferno shooting fiery tendrils into cold, black air and seeing — nothing. Blank night.

Sometimes in the middle of gigs, between songs, when everyone was tuning, he would look out into the dim theater, expecting to see the hot fire of a metal crowd and instead see that night. The anxiety would swell in those moments, the choking memories releasing their grip only when the band ripped into the next track.

Screaming lyrics about binding demons to go to war for you was easiest in those moments. He'd feel the mass heat of the crazed crowd on his chest and legs, the same way he had felt the fire in the ritual chamber that night, the licking flames that had grown and consumed the building. Closing in on him.

"That's why I needed to get a hold of you," Nick was saying. Brock blinked back the blur of daydream, felt himself coming back to the booth, to Nick's searching eyes.

"Sorry, I missed that," Brock said.

Nick saw Brock, one of the murderers of Floriana Gonzalez-Sanchez, a man who was out here in the world, among us, enjoying the fruits of music success, come back from his reverie, thinking, *this little rock star, staring doe-eyed at the building, day-dreaming of wearing his tight little pants and doing what? Just making this noise?* He took another sip of coffee and hoped its bitterness would drown out his own.

"What were you saying?" Brock asked.

"Horace Pantalione."

"Daathioz," Brock said.

"Daphne—" Nick said. "No, Horace. Pantalione."

Brock laughed, and Nick tensed. "Daathioz, like the sphere on the Tree of Life," he said. "Imagine your name being Horace Pantalione."

"I don't follow," Nick said.

"He called himself 'Daathioz.'"

"Can you spell that for me?" Nick asked. He had no pen or paper, but he knew this was an actual thing private investigators say and do.

"D, A, A, T," Brock started. "Hey, you're not writing this down."

"Nothing gets out of here," Nick said, pointing to his temple.

"You didn't remember my last name, man," Brock said, leaning back into the tall-backed teal couch.

Nick felt him fading away again. "He's dead," Nick said, trying to use surprise and regain the upper hand.

"You're not really a private investigator, are you, man?"

"Drug overdose," Nick said, trying the emotional trick again.

"Look, I hung out with that dude twice, once before and once after. Both at his place. The first time, his apartment was full of crystals; the second time, it was full of crystal. You get me? I'm surprised he lasted this long."

"After what?"

"I remember watching him take four hits while I stood there. I kept waiting for his nervous system to shake itself out of his skin. Then I left. Never seen him since."

"Before and after what?" Nick asked again, hoping Brock didn't notice the corner he'd just backed himself into. Brock looked at him, got up, crossed the aisle to the little bus kitchen, and started some tea. Nick let him, admiring the grace he moved with, his familiarity with the tour bus, knowing exactly what drawer was what. The instant kettle hissed to life.

"When this goes off, I'm pouring my tea for warm-ups and you're getting out of here," Brock said.

"You warm up to make the noise you make?"

"Especially to make the noise we make." The kettle hissed a little more insistently.

Nick stared at Brock for a moment and decided to close in. "What were you doing out there?" he asked.

"Out where?"

"Out where they found Floriana."

"Who is Floriana?" Brock asked, ripping the wrapper open and dropping the tea bag into a cup, insolently.

Nick exploded. "You know goddamn well who she is, or you wouldn't have talked to me. I saw your face when I said her name. That's how I knew it was you, you little shit."

"So, you're not a cop, and you're not a private investigator; you were fucking her, weren't you?" Brock smiled.

Nick leapt across the small aisle and grabbed Brock by his jacket. A small black pin with a white pentagram on the collar popped open and stuck Nick's finger. The wince of pain spiked his rage.

"Listen! We know what happened out there!" spittle flecking wet against the black leather. Nick didn't hear the thump of boots, just stared Brock in the eyes, and tried to find the exact words to cause the maximum preferred effect. He opened his mouth and felt hands grab his shoulders, yank him backward, and then he was slammed into the wall of the stairs. He grabbed for a handrail and aimed his voice towards the center of the bus.

"We know what you did! We know you killed her!" Nick shouted. "I have papers—" and then he was falling. He landed hard, heels of his boots hitting the pavement a second before his ass did. Two huge men grabbed him under his arms, lifted him up, and dragged him away from the bus.

Nick watched the bus recede, curtains drawing across the windows, then he felt himself tossed, the metal of a car door rising up to meet him.

THREE

The scotch left a water-ring as he picked it up, a droplet falling from the sweating glass that barely missed the open book. Nick wiped the water from the table with his sleeve, scooted the book a little further away from the moist smear, and looked at the page again, drawings of six demons with handwriting scroll under the pictures. One of those drawings had been crossed out completely with black sharpie, leaving an eye-catching, semi-gloss vacancy in the middle of the page. Nick tried holding the book under different angles of light to figure out what Horace had blacked out so completely.

Brock had called him "Daathioz." Nick's file said Horace. He was dead now, but Nick held both names in mind as he replayed the previous nights.

Nick had found him in a stroke of luck while walking downtown on his way to a restaurant. He had just happened to glance into an alley, as two men finished an exchange disguised as a handshake. One of them looked him in the eye, something in his face almost pleading, the pentagram tattooed on the side of the man's cheek a dead giveaway. A book bag bounced against the man's hip as he quickly slunk away, too new and incongruous against the rags of clothing.

Nick chased after him and watched Horace duck into a tent. But when Nick peered into the small tunnel of shredded, dingy fabric, there was no one there. Nick had batted at the nylon, looking for a hole or another zipper that someone could slip out of, left perplexed when he found nothing.

Nick returned over the next two nights to stake out the tent city. He brought along all the files and pictures Flor's brother had collected before giving up. The first night, he just watched Horace return to his tent. When he looked around in his paranoid surveillance Nick was able to match him to the picture, upside-down star on his sunken left cheek. A flash of flame illuminated a silhouette through the thin fabric. Then the opening of the tent unzipped at speed, and the bundle that contained Horace stomped off into the night. Nick tried to follow him on foot, but too many bums called out to him with questions, and he didn't want any suspicion, so he'd left.

The next night, he watched the same routine but Horace didn't come out. After too long, his nerves jumping, Nick had approached the tent and paused before the strong smell of burning plastic. He rattled the tent in a facsimile of knocking and got no response. When he opened it, the foul-smelling fog shrouded a non-responsive body, and Nick waited for the bundle to jump up and scare the shit out of him. When it didn't, Nick carefully unfolded the sleeping bag to reveal a face and lips already bluing.

Horace was dead, and Nick freaked. He decided not to move the body, but grabbed a stack of books and a tattered notebook. In his haste to stand, the weight clutched to his chest caused him to stumble, landing face to face with a shriveled corpse. *Like a prune*, Nick thought, and made too much noise trying to get out of the tent before the dread rose from its sleeping bag and chased him down, trying to get the books back. Only halfway down the block did he realize he had forgotten to close the tent.

He hadn't wanted to tell Brocken that Horace Daathioz was dead, but, in his desperation, he had. He wasn't sure if anyone else knew. How could they? Did the police even know?

Another sip of scotch, the blob of black ink somehow larger and slightly pulsing as he closed the book.

Brock was on stage, sweating. The band was between songs at a place in the set when he usually said something dumb about total support to the local black magicians and malign sorcerers, followed by a "Hail Satan." He heard the usual chuckle move through the crowd, the drummer making the appropriate jingle on the hats.

"Hail Satan," Brock said again, and then inadvertently hailed something else. The name came into his mind and passed through his mouth, and then he stopped, dumbfounded. He'd never said it out loud before, and he heard it pass through the PA system like knives of ice.

Brock looked out into the dim-lit house, but where there should have have been fans, there was the darkness and a copse of trees instead.

The fire in the building that night had been wild, almost rabid, and, in the parking lot, he'd stopped, looking back to the building to see the flames chewing their way through. He remembered clearly how bright it had been, how the eaves had been glowing red when Jared tore out of the parking lot. Halfway down the road, Brock had looked back again and seen nothing. Where there should have been a fire clawing into the sky, there was nothing but cold, torpid night.

Brock watched in horror as the vision of the flames assaulting the ritual chamber burst through his vision. He was standing center stage, frozen, as the opening riff ignited through the crowd and sent them launching into each other. The stage-lights had come back on, and the flame of the bulbs lit the front of the crowd in orange. His vocal chords moved the lyrics through his mouth automatically, but he was back *there* again, and the fire was consuming her body, and Jared was pulling him through the splintered door, and there was night where there should have been fire.

Halfway through the song, Brock knew he was doomed.

FOUR

It was the third scotch that gave Nick the confidence to put the book in front of Brock and demand new answers. As he pulled up to the venue, he realized he had no plan for getting inside, so he took the closest spot to the buses he could find and waited for the show to end.

Floriana would have known these drawings; he could have just asked her. She always loved that magick shit. "With a K," she always said. Light-headed with the booze, he drifted into soft, fuzzy memory. Her skin, her lips, her hair, her warmth.

But if he could have asked her now, he wouldn't be here at all.

The back door of the venue flew open, and sweat-drenched men poured out, white terrycloth towels around their heads or draped over their shoulders, one or two girls in tow. Nick saw Brock at the back accept a joint distractedly, his face long and vacant and haunted. Despite the adrenaline and the scotch, Nick resisted the impulse to jump from the car and run for him, yelling and shaking a stolen book in his face. He did grab the book, but he shut the car door as silently as he could and strode up to the group.

"Hey, our biggest fan," John said, spitting on the asphalt.

Brock's eyes went too wide too quickly, and Nick knew then that Brock knew. But John was in front of him, stopped Nick with a solid hand to the chest. John opened his mouth to speak, but Brock's voice was the one in the air.

"Show me," Brock said.

Nick's finger had been in the page, and he opened it, holding the black blob up to Brock.

"Where'd you get this?"

"This is one of only four earthly possessions that Horace left behind. He's dead, like I told you. Can you—" Nick stopped the question, re-formed it. "Tell me what this is and why it's blacked out," but the attempt at command came without the requisite force, jumbled with the desperation of the original question.

"I said its name on stage tonight," Brock said. For a moment, he stared straight ahead at the ground, then hunched over and retched.

"*What's* name?"

Brock disappeared around a corner of the bus, and Nick followed him.

"*What's* name?"

"Ok, time to leave," John said from behind him. John waved at the two muscled guys, who had introduced themselves to Nick earlier.

"*What's* name? Tell me, Brock! I need to know what's going on here!" Nick's voice was shaking now. The muscled guys had reached him, and he pointed at them, backing up. "Wait! Just wait! I'll leave. I'll leave! But I want him to at least answer that!"

Brock vomited again, and John nodded at the two large men. They grabbed Nick and picked him up. He kicked his legs, trying to find the ground. They dragged him to his car, threw him to the ground, and the blows came before he even hit the asphalt.

Nick quickly turned his head and brought his arms up to avoid what looked like an oncoming head-kick, and from that position, he could see that Brock was still doubled over, heaving. He cringed, waiting for the blow, but it never came.

Instead, he raised his head to see the men returning to the buses. Nick had guessed correctly that the guys were going just hard enough to make sure he got the message. His ribs would ache tomorrow, and he could feel an eye puffing up. Message received.

Nick climbed slowly into his car and started it. The rearview mirror said his nose was bleeding. He sighed, punched the steering wheel with an impotent yell as the pain from rock-scraped palms reported back, and then grabbed the notebook next to him. The next name under Brock's was Hakim Raphelson, with an address two states over, probably twelve hours of driving. He threw the notebook against the passenger door and stifled a sob.

John was helping Brock onto the bus, and Nick was in receipt of nothing, just more questions. He started the car and backed up, not turning the lights on until he was pointing away from the tour buses.

FIVE

Brocken lay in his bunk and tried to breathe through the anxiety. The bong rips were not the best idea; after the third one, his mind became stuck on rewatching Flor's vital essence drain into the candlelit air. He waited for the top of the high to descend, the sharp nausea and stomach pain to round out a bit.

What happened on stage tonight: the presence of a presence, the oxygen sucked from the room, the lights around the periphery drowned in liquid dark, echoed that night in the circle.

And he'd said the name out loud.

He remembered catching a fish when he was young. Brock had marveled at the way the sun glinted off its thrashing body. His friend, Jimmy, had told him to reach out and grab it, so he'd stretched out and clamped his hand around the slimy middle, but when his fist clenched, the fish shot straight up into the air. Brock thought it had suddenly learned to fly, and then felt an ugly vibration from the fishing rod as the still-hooked fish fell and bounced on the line. The name had slipped out of his mouth just like that fish had slipped out of his hand.

He felt a drop of sweat furrow down his side, other drops following its path. He had a slight cramp in his stomach, so he shifted uncomfortably in the small bunk and thought of how Flor had lain; twisted, gnarled, mummified, when just minutes before, she had been a tantalizing erotic energy, vibrant and full of life. The ritual itself was a blur. The only other thing he really remembered from that night was his van breaking down and Jared picking him up.

Brocken had left the hood of the dying van open and tried to divine from the patterns of acrid-smelling smoke and hissing steam.

How is this going to go for me? He sent his query to the spirits of the broken motor, then waited and watched. When nothing happened, he tried to light a joint, but his lighter didn't work. Frustrated, he turned his back to the smoking censer of the van and abandoned his attempts at capnomancy. A quick survey of the empty surrounding area told him the mountains weren't visible this far east. The world was so flat here you could see the Earth start to curve: where he should have been able to see everything, he saw vast distances of nothing; flat grass wasteland. Except for one tiny copse of trees in the distance.

A very dark doubt quickly sprung in his mind, the van and lighter a bad omen. The lighter subtly trembled in his hand as he tried it again. When it didn't spark, he closed his eyes and sighed, hoping for something to give him a sign that this whole thing wasn't a terrible idea.

He heard the car before he saw it.

Brocken held the joint out like a hitchhiking thumb. The car slowed, and he flicked the lighter again. Impotent spark. Yellow flash against the darkening sky, a hand extending out of the passenger window, offering vital flame. Brocken leaned over it, inhaled, and lit the weed.

"Hey, shit man, this one escaped," the passenger said. A decent beard against black clothes.

"Hey man, some farmer up the road said his sheep got out of the pen; why don't you hop in, so we can bring you back to the flock?" the driver said. A lesser beard, long silver hair with gentle features, and a bright, calming smile.

"Yeah, get back in the car," the passenger said, bleating like a sheep.

Brock's voice was husky with the exhale. "Who the fuck is this guy?"

"The extra. Get in, man."

"Can I smoke this in there?"

"No way, man," the driver said, pulling out a trident-shaped piece of wood, a joint in all three ends. "We only smoke *this* in the car."

"Fucking Jared, man," Brock said, laughing and climbing into the back seat. The car smelled like weed, and he pretzeled himself around the various boxes and containers.

"How you doing, man? This is Mike," Jared said, passing the joints. Mike lifted his hand in greeting from the passenger seat. "Hey, what happened to your band van?"

Brock took the trident. "Broke down. Our last tour fucked us. We kept the transmission together with straws and incantations, and I think today we lay her to rest," he said. "The dudes are gonna be so pissed at me."

"So, you're just gonna leave it there with all the memories?" Jared asked.

"Memories and the odor of gas station burrito and sour dudes. «

"Fasting for three days makes a gas station burrito sound good as hell," Jared said.

"Wait, have you guys actually been doing the fasting?" Mike said.

Jared braked the car, hard. "You said you hadn't eaten."

"You better have been fucking fasting too," Brock started.

"I forgot until Jared said something," Mike said.

"You better be fucking kidding me," Jared said.

If this shit doesn't work— " Brock said.

"If you're serious, man—" Jared said.

"If I'm serious, then what?" Mike said. "What are you gonna do?"

"Then I drive you back to the burrito band wagon and you can wait until we're done," Jared said.

Brock felt the bad omen push down on him again.

"I've been doing it, guys, just razzing you," Mike said. Jared gave him a silent moment's look, and then started to drive again, and Mike added, "Wow, you guys take this really seriously, don't you?"

"If you do certain things right, certain things happen," Jared said. The car did a slight wobble between the two lanes of the road as he reached backwards to take the trident.

"What the fuck does that mean?" Mike said. The car swung toward the copse of trees, and its headlights illuminated a weed-ridden parking lot. Nothing and a parking lot, Brocken thought.

"We've been putting this together for a year, man. If this doesn't work cause someone wanted to do some mundane shit, like eat—" Jared said, parking.

"Or fuck," Brocken said. "You haven't fucked, have you?"

"Nah, man," Mike said, hands conciliatory. "But there were some sheep back there."

Brock got up and walked towards the front of the bus, holding his aching stomach. He stopped at the kitchen and stared out the window. The only view was black movement as the bus throttled to the next city. The bus. And the one behind them.

For a moment, Brock marveled; he was a touring death metal musician, and his band had gotten big enough in their small scene to quit their jobs. Two critically acclaimed albums and tours with some of their heroes. Rabid fans, drugs, alcohol, sometimes even chicks. Good times and blast beats. It was an absolute thrill, even for the twenty-two hours a day they weren't onstage, slogging through drives or sitting around for countless hours in empty venues.

It's what he'd asked for.

He wasn't living in a mansion, but he wasn't driving in a van. Plenty of tours and plenty of off-time for hobbies; reading, occult practice, band rehearsal, groupies, collecting music and merch. His living expenses were paid, he had a decent house with his best friends, they all had sponsorships: an upward arc of a career. He'd gotten word-for-word, line-for-line, exactly what he'd asked for.

He turned to face the back of the bus, heard people in the large back room watching a movie and fucking around. He fought the nausea, opened a cabinet labeled "puking supplies," and grabbed a plastic bag.

The thing had wanted only one thing in exchange: for them to keep completely silent. To not be disturbed while it relished its gift. In the dark porthole of the bus window, he saw it conjured again — Flor's beautiful, naked body on the altar, sucked dry.

There had been a perceptible, tactile shockwave of desire when the thing had seen what they gifted it. Telepathically, its exposed eagerness, its naked thoughts and horrors beyond comprehension had bloomed in Brock's mind like summer fruit.

He shivered as he climbed into the small cubby that contained his bed, stomach twitching with the movement. As his hand closed the small accordion curtain of his bunk, he glanced at the tattoo on it, the evil-looking Sphinx. To remind him of the Four Powers of the Sphinx: To Know, To Will, To Dare, and To Keep Silent. He had done all of those until tonight, when the name slipped from his tongue like a receding ocean tide. The thing had entered his mind, mean and big.

It wanted hundreds of years alone with the sacrifice, and they couldn't last four.

Daathioz was dead, and this Nick guy knew something. The bile in his throat rose again, pain in his belly like being poked with something sharp when he thought about Nick, about the book and its blacked-out blob smack in the middle of the page, and how he had waved it around madly.

Brock lay on his back, sweating and sick to his stomach, and waited for his tour manager to slide the curtain back and tell him the tour had been cancelled. Record deal lost. House foreclosed. His bandmates would point accusing fingers and kick him out and leave him on the side of the road on their way to the next city, where his replacement would board the bus and empty his bunk eagerly. He waited for everything he'd gained to be stripped from him, everything he desired, everything he wanted out of life to be confiscated and burned in a pyre in front of him.

He turned onto his side, the pain fleeing for a blessed moment, and considered the possibility that none of this was real, maybe that night had just been a horrible accident or a vivid dream; he would wake up from this night terror in the small bed in his parents' stuffy attic. Or maybe all of the magick stuff was bullshit, and he'd gained all of this on his own, no help from the astral realms, no assistance from spirits or gods. No help meant no consequences of a broken pact, and he'd get to keep it all.

He twisted onto his other side, the empty cramp in his stomach growing, hurting. He tried breathing again, focusing, thinking of something else. The only memory his mind presented him was their narrow escape.

Jared, Brocken, and Mike had gotten into Jared's car and had it running. The fire ripped through the building, tearing through holes it had eaten in the roof, and was painfully bright, enough that Brock was squinting when he saw Hakim finally drag Daathioz outside and into Jackie's car. Jackie's eyes were wide with horror, wet with tears, and he could see her mouth opening. He couldn't hear her through the closed windows, but he figured she was probably screaming.

"Let's get the fuck out of here!" Mike's voice, too loud in the car, yelling at Jared, shaking the driver's seat. Brock didn't remember Jared leaving, didn't remember anything until they were down the road, and he found himself staring into the flat, empty distance, turning around to look back at the copse of trees, waiting to see how big the towering fire was. He heard nothing in the car, saw nothing in the distance.

And then the next memory: Jared waking him up in front of his apartment.

His stomach was throbbing now, and the small space of the bunk was too warm. Brock turned again and lay on his back. Above him, taped to the ceiling, was a mandala he had gotten from a street vendor in Nepal when they played Kathmandu Death Fest. He stared at it and tried to even his breathing.

The mandala began to bend and twist sickeningly. Clammy sweat hastened from his brow, and he felt his stomach distend as the pain turned a corner. Brock craned his neck up, forehead hitting the top of the bunk, straining his eyes down and forward to his belly button. His horror screened the agony, but barely — the center of his stomach was rising into the air, and he thought again of the fish, the way the hook had pulled its mouth forward and out, unnaturally extending its lower lip.

Something pulled abruptly at his belly, and he watched it inch impossibly outwards and up. The sweat on his forehead dampened, and his vision oscillated, dizzy with the pain. He yanked open the curtain to get some air. The movement caused horrible discomfort, and he gagged. The air he hoped to circulate was tepid, unmoving.. The lights of the bus were off, and there swirled darkness. The pain was stropped as he sat up to vomit, elbow against soaked bedding. He remembered the beauty of the brass candelabrum outside the circle, and Brock tried to scream, to curse Nick for showing him the picture. But no sound came, and he knew the deal.

A feeling from his navel, like it was dripping water. He gagged again and felt the vomit catch in his throat. His stomach tightened like a vise, and he began to choke on the trapped liquid. The pain intensified, his vision turning white and fuzzy when he looked and saw his stomach extending further away from him, coning out like carpet being sucked by a vacuum cleaner, rubbing now against the ceiling of his bunk.

He tried to force his core to expel the puke but had no control, no ability to push against the agony. He felt his shoulders pinned down, his spine digging into the wet mattress as something inside of him began to yank.

His last thought: I can't even cry. Then, his consciousness flickered, and his essence was sucked from him, steadily slurped like noodles into a malefic ethereal gullet. After a final protracted throb, Brocken's body lay suddenly still, shrunken and hollow. There was no gore, no mess, no explosion of meat and flesh against the ceiling. His shrunken, wrinkled body lay there calm, but his spirit had screamed the whole time.

The bus driver was opening his flask to pour a little bit more into his coffee and didn't have time to get his hands back on the wheel when the curve was suddenly ahead of him.

Brock's spirit, gripped and dragged backwards by claws of primordial cold, watched through a shrinking tunnel of dark as the bus headed towards the cliff. No brake lights illuminated.

When he heard Floriana screaming, he started, too.

According to the analogue clock on the dashboard, Nick was seven hours into his drive when the radio informed him of two tour buses that had missed a curve and plunged hundreds of feet down a mountain pass, killing everyone aboard. Nick was suddenly aware of the saliva in his mouth, and when he tried to swallow, he gulped. The feeling like hot liquid going down the wrong pipe in his throat overwhelmed him, and he swooned in the still air of the car.

He watched his hands move from far away, like they weren't even his, shutting off the radio. After a few moments, the warm dizziness fled, and the highway noise filled the air around him as he returned to his body.

Just to see if he could move of his own volition, he pulled the next file folder onto his lap. Hakim's home address was written on a sticky note underneath a much better quality picture than Brock's; less fuzz, closer, and sharper.

Nick tried to concentrate on the details of the face, but the picture doubled, and Nick brought his attention back to the headlights and the white lines rushing towards him, stretching, receding.

Six

From the roundabout driveway, the house looked modest, set back on a large yard. After two unanswered rings and loud knocks on the oversized oak door, Nick turned back to face his car, picked a direction, and started walking.

As he got further around the side of the house, the outbuildings came into view and revealed the depth and scope of the place — a tall, white fence he took to be the property line extended as far as he could see, before it sloped over the rolling, wooded hills in the distance and vanished. He let himself into a small latched gate, suddenly light-headed as he stepped through.

He was careful to step over rows of well-manicured flowers and plots of small plants and onto the smooth, paved stone walkways that led in different directions across the lush yard. *Hardly a yard*, Nick thought. More like a grounds. If Flor could have seen this place, she would have gotten that special twinkle in her eye, the one she got when she was denoting the varieties of wealthy cultural details. Nick could almost hear her husky purr, asking him if he knew the difference between a yard and a grounds.

He shifted the file folder between hands as his eyes scanned the length and direction of the outlined trails: one leading to a building that looked like a barn, one to a fenced-in square with tall, sagging plants in the middle of it, which Nick took for a garden of sorts, and one path looked to lead to a plain white building in a circle of trees. Movement in the garden split the stillness.

"A private private investigator," he said, practicing. He stepped from the shade of the fruit trees that followed the large white pickets in perfect lines out into the far distance. He felt the sunlight and let his skin absorb it.

By the time he got to the garden, he felt like he'd been walking all morning, though he must have just underestimated the distance. An angular, handsome black face, smiling at him from tall, perfect rows of corn, re-sharpened his awareness. Nick felt the muscles on the side of his head tighten and pull back, the air on his teeth suggesting that he was grinning back. The unfamiliarity of that feeling caught Nick mid-stride.

"Yo, can I help you?" the man said, laying a hoe against a waist-high white-washed wooden slat fence.

"Nick Kyle, private private investigator. I'm looking for Hakim, uh—" and Nick looked down at the file for help.

Instead of the folder, his hand held the book. He inadvertently swallowed the lump that had appeared in his throat. "I'm looking for Hakim," he said, coughing through the choking feeling. He tried to minimize his shift in posture as he slid the book slowly out of view, but Hakim was already moving his eyes back up to Nick's; the look in them changed to less friendly.

"That's me," the man in the garden said. He raised gloved hands, curved symmetry of large forearm muscles catching the sun, then set them to rest on the posts of the garden fence.

Big, juicy-looking fruits hung heavily from the plants. Large leaves glowed with ethereal green, with none of the telltale holes of insect predation or disease. Everything was in straight rows, perfect and equivalent, edged on all sides with huge, pristine sunflowers and marigolds. No brown, no signs of wilt or decay. The flowers stood proud, upright at perfect attention, absorbing their noonday food.

"You have a beautiful garden," Nick said.

Hakim laughed and said a word that Nick didn't catch. Nick suddenly remembered why he had driven all this way, his mind clearing from a strange onset of fog.

"It's a very enchanting garden, for sure," Hakim said with a wry smile.

"I'm here to ask you about Horace Pantalione, aka Daathioz," Nick said, remembering the lingo. He felt relief as his voice firmed.

"Why's that?"

"I have some information about him and you're a known associate of his," Nick said, then waited in the prolonged silence for Hakim to decide.

"Last time I saw him, he took a few of my books and left out a window," Hakim said. "Expensive ones."

Compelled, Nick raised the book into view. "Was this one of 'em?" Nick said.

"Nope," Hakim said, letting it hang in the air. "Burned my copy of that."

Nick felt the sun leave the back of his neck as it passed behind a cloud. "Isn't it illegal to burn books?"

Behind them, a dog barked, and Nick turned. Two huge French doors at the back of the house were open, curtains flowing in the soft breeze. Towards them, at rapid speed, ran a fluffy white sheep dog with three little girls chasing it. They reached Nick much quicker than he thought they should — he remembered that walk taking forever. The girls stopped short at the sight of the stranger, while the dog circled Nick, sniffing. When he held the book up out of the dog's reach, Hakim grabbed it. A melodious voice floated from the house and across the lawn.

"Girls!"

Nick tried, doubtful. "Good morning, girls."

"Go with Mom and get the saddles ready," Hakim said. They needed no further prodding. At their first steps, the dog was on their heels, barking and herding them back to the house. In the sudden absence of the noise, Nick heard pages shuffling.

"Where'd you get this?" Hakim asked, the book open, sun shining harshly off a blot of black ink. Nick felt a quick chill, but none of the leaves had blown in a breeze.

"Horace has died. Is dead." Nick said, fixing the tense and finishing as gravely as he could. "I have reason to believe that Brock Ericsson has died, too."

From the goosebumps on his arms, Nick guessed that Hakim registered the information, but the look on his face was distant.

"Babe, are you ok?" a woman said behind Nick. Nick turned again, and it was like someone had inverted the scene. The woman, tall, solid, and beautiful, stood behind him now, and the girls framed the door of the house, the dog sitting with the littlest of them.

"Who are you? What are you doing here?" she asked Nick.

"Nick Kyle, private priv—" he started.

"I have to talk to this guy, Danta," Hakim said.

"About what?"

"Give me half an hour and tell the girls we'll ride down to the creek as soon as I'm done." He put a cupped hand to the side of his mouth and shouted over Nick's shoulder. "Those horses aren't gonna saddle themselves!"

Nick saw Hakim's other hand holding the book behind his back as casually as he could.

"Danta, can you go help them?" Hakim asked. She shifted her calculation to Nick for a long moment. "Please."

Danta turned, audibly miffed, and walked back towards the house.

"Nice to meet you, ma'am," Nick said. The sun came back out, warmth announcing itself with the sound of the garden latch sliding open, illuminating Hakim as he strode towards Nick. Shango in battle triumph. He wondered if he and Floriana had ever?

"This way," Hakim said, moving down a path to the plain white building.

SEVEN

It was much bigger inside than it had looked from the garden. Before Nick's eyes, the walls cowered backwards, withdrawing from his presence and leaving puddles of crepuscular air in their wake. "No power to the building," said Hakim, lighter igniting in his hand.

"No windows, either," Nick said.

Hakim lit a few candles, and their glow magnified as the wicks caught. The orange flame danced across the room to a wall of books, some of which looked very old.

"I do a lot of my work out here, away from the kids." Hakim set a candelabra down on a table in the middle of the room, fanning dry powders off the top and moving a few tools neatly to the far edge. The candlelight was strong enough to illuminate other tables and cabinets lining one wall and stocked bookshelves lining the other. Nick couldn't see the ends of the room.

"I make talismans and shit," Hakim said, dusting his hands off. The motes of dust formed a cloud as they left his hands and, in the orange glow, Nick thought he saw a symbol coalesce. *Flor would know*, he thought, then the last glimpse of the dust brought him back to the reverie of that day at the beach.

"Okay, this one works, I guess," Hakim said, laughing. "I'm glad you came out today: I was wanting to test something. Have a seat."

"Test something?" But instead of an answer, Hakim set the book between them. He then opened a drawer and withdrew a small pair of antique scissors. The scissors looked heavy, but the sound of them against the table sounded muffled. Hakim reached above him and grabbed for something. Nick's decision to do this unarmed felt suddenly like a poor one, and he followed the movement up, mouth dry.

From improbably high rafters hung different dry herbs, tied together in bouquets, most of the visible ceiling covered with them. Nick thought of bundled bodies hung upside down. He pictured Flor and wondered if these people had tied her up in a sack like that.

Herbs in his hand now, Hakim began snipping the roots off, and then asked, "Do you know what valerian is good for?"

"I'm here because Horace and Brock are dead and I want answers," Nick said, surprised at the sudden rush of confidence.

"You're not a cop," Hakim said, snipping.

"I'm not a cop," Nick said. "I'm a private— "

"Private investigator. You said that." Nick watched bits of plant fall and land on the book between them. Hakim brushed them absently onto the table, leaving a smear of powder across the cover, then blew the remaining dust off and a foul-smelling cloud enveloped Nick, climbing his sinuses and watering his eyes. "But that's not true, is it?" Hakim threw a stem behind him and started snipping another. The gold ring on his middle finger caught a ray of candlelight and threw it across the far wall.

"I've been hired by the family of Floriana Gonzalez-Sanchez to investigate."

"To investigate what?"

"Her disappearance," Nick said, waiting for a reaction. Hakim became more careful snipping. "And murder," Nick added for effect.

"Flor's family hired you, huh?" Hakim ignored the effect. "They hired you to find Daathioz, too, then?"

"They did."

"They didn't, though, because they didn't know about Daathioz," Hakim said, the scissors increasing in speed.

"I found out about Horace," said Nick, caught.

"Daathioz."

"Daathioz," Nick repeated, following Hakim's lead. "Through her family."

"You were fucking her, weren't you?"

Nick's voice dropped the word it was about to form, and Hakim laughed, put the scissors down, and used a forearm to sweep some chopped remains into a pile, stopping to shake with laughter. "Were you with her before she disappeared?"

"I'm here on behalf of the Gonzalez-Sanchez fa—"

"You're here cause some sweet pussy disappeared, and she probably did enough sex magick with you to make it really burn."

Nick had a scene from his memory with Flor flash through his mind. His pants tightened, and he swallowed unconsciously. Hakim caught it and laughed.

"Tell me about the book," Nick said. Hakim took an herb grinder out of the drawer, replaced the scissors, and slammed it shut. Nick jumped despite himself, regretting it instantly. Hakim began loading the grinder and clamped the lid on. After the first tug of resistance, Nick saw Hakim's forearms flex and bulge, turning the grinder easily. Metal scraped against metal, and Nick felt like prey being sized up.

"Nah," Hakim finally said, then mouthed something Nick didn't catch. Another few twists, and he opened the lid, dumped the contents into a mason jar. "Nah," he said again and laughed. "Tell me about sex magick with Flor. Or you gonna keep lying?"

Abruptly, a load lifted from Nick's shoulders. He felt light and at ease, and he wondered if Hakim would come out later and have a drink with him. "It was unreal," he said through soft, hazy, and suddenly present memories of Flor.

Hakim laughed again, stuck the lid of the jar halfway on without tightening it. "Something tells me you're not lying. When were you with her?"

"We went to Italy, she ran around to all these weird places and antique dealers. She disappeared the night we got home," Nick said. He wasn't comfortable sharing any of this with Hakim, but something drew it out of him. "I've never—"

"You've never what? Gotten over it? Had better head?"

"Gotten over it," Nick said, and heard his voice float up a half-step on a wave of despondence. "Where is she?"

Hakim stopped, then loaded more chopped herbs. "Believe me when I say, you don't wanna know, and I can't tell you."

"But this book has something to do with it?" Nick opened the book to the now well-thumbed page and its blacked-out block of text. Hakim looked at it once quickly, and Nick was too slow to react when his arm shot out. The sound of the book slamming shut and the flash of terror on Hakim's face unmoored Nick. His anxiety welled back up: why had he told Hakim all that? What was he thinking, giving that much away? The ease had fled the room, replaced by the sharp edges of stress, the open pit of uncertainty. Nick became aware of the wet cotton under his arms, felt the sweat run down his side.

Hakim had a lighter in his other hand now, and its flame flashed suddenly. Nick jumped across the table when Hakim raised the book up to the glow, tips of fingers grasping, somehow yanking it away.

"Give me that book," Hakim said, his charm and confidence replaced by some darker presence of anger radiating out and filling the room.

"No, I need it. It's evidence, I'm —"

Hakim lunged at Nick, who jumped back to evade him. Hakim missed and stopped in the middle of an awkward stumble. "You're not any of that. I came from nothing, and I have everything, and you're not going to take anything from me."

"How does me having a book take everything from—" Nick started, stopping mid-sentence as the horror rose within him. "The figure that's blacked out is what Flor was—"

"Give me the book and give this up," Hakim growled. His eyes were wild, too bright now. "You are making this worse for her. You are going to make this so much worse for her," he said, stifling a sob. "It's so bad already, and you're going to make it so much worse for her and us."

"Tell me what this is about, maybe I can help you. Maybe we can help each other."

"I can't. *I literally cannot!*" Hakim shouted. The ceiling above him burgeoned upwards, lifted, and bowed with the shout. Then he said, softer. "We made a pact." As he took a step forward, arm and hand extended in a gesture of reception, Nick took a step back. Hakim sighed and then squared his body to Nick's. No air passed through the room, yet the candle guttered.

"You're not going to find her. She's — gone."

"What do you mean, gone?"

"We should take this outside, into the sunlight," Hakim said. Neither of them moved. Nick eyed Hakim, who loomed in the half-light and filled his entire field of vision, then glanced to where he thought the exterior door should be. It wasn't there. Hakim dusted his hands and walked towards the wall. At his presence, the cracks of the door appeared, edges glowing. Hakim pushed and flooded the room with sunlight. Nick had no reason to believe it wouldn't open, but he found himself relieved.

Where a moment ago Hakim's presence filled the room, he looked normal in the doorway now, the angry grief gone from his face. Nick shuffled sideways into the afternoon, trying simultaneously to keep the book away from Hakim and not scratch it on the frame.

After the dark room, the sunlight was blinding, and Nick held his hands up, using the book as a visor to dim the fading discomfort. Quickly and awkwardly, he scrambled onto the lawn, trying to put space between himself and Hakim.

"You can't burn it, it's evidence." The sunlight and warmth on his back gave Nick a little boost of confidence, and he turned the cop-talk dial up.

"Evidence of what?"

"Murder."

"It wasn't murder."

"Then what was it?"

"It was everything we wanted," Hakim said. He looked around. "We got everything we ever wanted."

"Where is Flor?"

"She got what she wanted, too."

"You fucking bastard! Where is she?" Nick tried tough cop, genuine rage assisting him into the role.

"I don't know. I really don't know. I don't even know if I want to know. And even if I did, do you think you're ready to hear?"

Nick ignored the question, trying not to hint that he knew he probably wasn't. "Tell me why this figure is blacked out."

"Give me the book, man. You don't want this smoke. I'll buy it from you. Right now. Twenty thousand dollars, cash." Hakim held his hand out. Nick saw the force of panic in Hakim's eyes, but the memory of the heat of Floriana's body against him was stronger.

"No, sir. This is evidence."

"Fifty thousand."

He stared at Hakim. "Tell me what's going on here, man."

"Get the fuck off my property," Hakim said, his face set in finality, strong in the half-sunlight of late afternoon. Behind him, through the shade-lines of tree branches thick with red fruit, Nick heard a bird call, the first he remembered in days.

On his way to the car, Nick tried to take inventory of what he'd been told. What they'd talked about. He found it was hard to remember, knew he had a long walk back, and would have the time to tease it out. Being in the building had been like being out of time. The sun was setting now, but had barely reached its apex when they'd stepped in. And yet, the conversation hadn't been long enough to cover that amount of daylight.

Then he was at his car, too quickly. He remembered how long the walk had taken when he'd arrived and crossed the yard to the garden, and it didn't match how rapidly he'd now returned to the driveway. Nick chalked it up to adrenaline and the testosterone that had leaked into the confined space.

The car door shut, key in the ignition. Nick looked up and out of the car to make sure no one had followed him, then wrapped the book back in its cloth, set it back in the bottom of his briefcase, and shuffled through identical folders until he found the next name on the list. She was in the same state, at least.

EIGHT

Hakim couldn't focus on dinner and headed outside as soon as the girls went to bed, thinking maybe some fresh air would help his headache.

Danta had planted a night-blooming jasmine outside the kitchen window, and its smell usually drifted indolently through the dusk air, a token example of her home-making and level, open-hearted energy. Hakim breathed in to try to catch its scent, but tonight he only smelled a sulphurous rot that hastened him to his workshop.

He'd been early that night to the ritual despite his intense doubts. Those same doubts returned tonight on tenebrous wings. He fumbled through his cargo pants for a lighter and its plastic certainty. It sparked briefly, illuminating the room. He crossed to the wall and turned on some lights, chuckling at what he'd told Nick. The harsh halogen left no refuge for malignant shadows to propagate, and he felt better under its beam, opening a cabinet where he kept his stash and papers.

He had the joint hanging from his lips when the lights went out. He rolled his thumb over the wheel, again and again, until finally it sparked. The flame danced in his jittering hands as the paper caught, and he used the burning end to find his way in the dark. When he lit a candle, his head throbbed with the flaring light. He used that candle to ignite another candle, then used that candle to light another. Despite their light, the dark of the room amplified — just like it had outside the circle that night.

Hakim had been the first one there. The drive was strange and long, cruise control at eighty-five untouched for the final two hours of the trip. The location of the place was in the middle of flat plains, totally barren surroundings. Then, in the far distance, he'd seen a lone stand of trees. When he'd finally pulled into the parking lot next to the decrepit building, he wondered what the fuck he was doing out here with these white people.

The second car arrived shortly after he did, with Jared, Brock, and some guy he'd never met before. Jared had greeted him with their usual handshake, and they'd started hauling boxes from the back of Jared's car towards the front door.

"We're the first ones here, I guess," Hakim had said.

"Typical," said Brocken. "You got the keys?"

"Someone's actually locking this place up?" the other guy asked.

Hakim fumbled with the key ring that Flor had been very serious about giving him, trying different keys in the first lock. One finally fit, and the lock clicked open. He grabbed the ornate handle and pushed, but the door didn't budge.

"Another lock right there," Brocken said, pointing to an older-looking keyhole below the first. Hakim found the right key, turned the lock, and tried the door again. This time, he pushed it with his shoulder. It didn't move, so he tried again, more aggressively.

"Bro, what the fuck?" Hakim said, stepping back. They all looked at the door, and then Jared pointed to another lock about a foot from the ground.

"Right there, at the bottom," Jared said. "A door for the gnomes, man."

Hakim knelt down and searched the keys again. When the lock slid free, it made a sound like finally getting a foot into a tight shoe. Hakim stood up, grabbed the handle, and looked at it, then put his shoulder to the door, stumbling a bit as the door slid easily inwards.

Together with the others, he peered through the doorway. The darkness inside aspirated, expanding and contracting, but he told himself his eyes were just adjusting.

"Don't just fuckin' stand there, guys, hand me a candle."

Jackie and Horace pulled up in Jackie's car right before they entered. Jackie had been frazzled by the drive, thinking she'd gotten lost. Hakim gave her a big hug and felt her calm a bit, glad to see her smile. Something about that smile tempered the building's grim aura.

The building only had two rooms: the first was large and circular, with dirty slate floors, rounded walls and an actively splintering wood door on the far side. They continued hauling in the boxes and setting them right inside the entrance of the triple locked door, and then the other guy — introduced as Mike — helped Jared carry the last thing in, a large and very heavy hardleather case.

Mike had let his side drop, and Jackie had very sternly admonished him to be more careful. "All of this is custom-made, brought in from Italy and other places. These are religious objects. Do try and treat them as such."

"She brought all this back from Italy?" Hakim asked as he opened the latches. He unwrapped the black silk coverings, astonished at the beauty of the wrought metal underneath.

"This all bronze?" Brocken asked in turn, tapping the edge of his gold ring on the metal, which clanged shrilly.

"I think some of it's gold," Jared answered, and then gestured towards the inner door. It opened, with no keys or sound, to a room nearly identical to the first, this one with squared-off walls and warmer, mustier air.

From their silence, Hakim could tell the others were also trying to adjust to the strange vertigo that warped over the threshold. Jared and Mike had both gone back to grab candles whose shine had been lessened by the way their hands were shaking. Even now, safe with time's distance and the bright lights of the shed, Hakim could feel the creep of the sensation, and his head swam with the memory.

At Flor's instruction, once the room had been lit, Hakim was to be left alone to set the circle. He'd almost asked if the others would stay, but Jared had hustled them out; something about Jared trusting him had given Hakim the confidence to begin. Three-quarters of the way around the cast circle, the boundaries began to take and shift the air into more positive possibilities. The doubts had started to give way to his assurance and self-confidence until he looked back to the eastern quadrant and saw wet footprints.

Hakim turned himself back to west, his heart loud in his ears. The south edge had the same footprints, but thicker and more pronounced. His suddenly dry mouth and throat croaked out the rest of the words of the banishing.

Hakim's right temple pounded now, remembering the way he had willed himself to continue, almost sprinting out of the room and forcing himself not to look back when he'd finished.

When he had gotten back to the others, Flor was there. He tried to play it cool in front of her, consciously forcing his eyes half-shut so no one would notice how wide they'd become once he'd seen that the footprints had followed him out.

He had thought the responsible thing to do was just to say it; to tell them, in case something dangerous was going on. But then, after rubbing his hands on his robe, he saw wet imprints. The soles of his feet felt cold and damp — he touched one of them and laughed: he'd made the tracks himself. When Jackie looked at him with the question in her face, he'd told the group about the footprints, and their chuckles quieted the tense air, lending a bit of ease to the atmosphere.

Hakim was still astonished at how quickly everything had deteriorated from there.

Before that night, he'd been practicing the occult for almost two decades and had seen all kinds of things: the demons of Solomon brought to visible appearance, angelic miracles honed through dreams. He'd seen physical, rippling electricity in the strange vistas of the Enochian Aethyrs, elementals dancing around him in the dark woods of national park campsites, and had far too many meetings in random hotel rooms with channeling cults. What had bubbled from Flor's mouth that night was just another in the long line of surprises magic had wrought, but he'd suspected it was fake. Sure, she had flailed a bit, putting on quite a good show — the ardor was as strong as he'd ever felt in ritual.

But he'd never seen anything like the shimmer.

He'd watched — and would never forget as long as he lived — something scintillating leave Flor and ascend towards the blurry black as it drank of her. And the next thing Hakim had seen was her body, withering like a time-lapse of drying fruit. He'd felt his mind slip then, felt himself almost lose it. The adrenaline kept him centered as they'd fled, but the long drive home had been a contest of his sanity.

The day after had almost been worse. He'd sat alone in his apartment and stared at the walls, catatonic. When the fugue finally abated, he was hungry, found nothing but some old pancake mix in the pantry and a jar of pickles in the fridge. He was two and a half aisles into shopping before the flint banality of the grocery store collided with the horror of what he'd seen. He escaped through the automatic doors before his psyche fragmented.

The strawberries he'd walked out with were completely molded when he woke the next day. In his involuntarily fasted state, he had logged on to his computer and thrown his rent money into stocks he'd selected by throwing a tarot spread. Looking back now, the subconscious attempt at self-destruction was clear to him, but a week later, one of the computer companies he'd invested in hit some kind of milestone in its search engine development. It closed on Thursday at a record-breaking high. The pundits were baffled. On Friday morning, Hakim woke up rich.

And then he threw himself headlong into the abyss of work. He invested, built up his portfolio, bought one property after another. Nothing ever went wrong. His investments grew, he knew when to sell, never had anything bottom-out on him. But no matter how big his bedrooms got or how beautiful the views they overlooked, he couldn't sleep. Every time he closed his eyes, he saw her leaving, watched her wither, crumple, implode in huge explosions of dust, and she cried and wept and screamed for him to help.

In the following months and then years, he tried everything: therapists, treatment, medication, spiritual baths, banishing rituals, whatever he could find. With some of his new money, he bribed the local Cardinal into Catholic exorcism. After three days of intensive prayers and rites, the priests left his sprawling house shaking their heads, the brake-lights of their new Cadillacs bright against the dawn.

He flew to Brazil for an initiation into Quimbanda, but the Tata rejected him. "Too dark," the Tata had said, and Hakim knew he wasn't referencing his skin color. Dejected in São Paulo/ Guarulhos International Airport, he bought another ticket to

Nepal, but found only Buddhist teachers with nothing more to offer than "Life is Suffering." Little did they know how long the suffering could actually continue.

At a dive bar one night, six months after he returned, his waitress introduced herself as Danta. When he'd looked into the green eyes, bright beneath her curly black hair, he'd felt a wave of calm wash over him for the first time in years. He took her out after her shift, and they'd walked aimlessly. Her voice was honey, and he held her hand like he was about to fall off a cliff. He proposed in the morning as they watched the sun come up on the beach. The first time she slept beside him in bed was the first time he slept through the night since the ritual.

It didn't stick though. He built Danta her dream house, and they'd started their family, but sleep was still fleeting, interrupted by week-long periods of insomnia where he'd wander through this huge house and across the beautiful orchards and gardens, wondering if he'd give it all back if it would make Flor stop begging him to save her.

Now, stoned in the dark room of his workshop lit by candles that gave hardly any illumination, Hakim tried to look around at all that he'd gained: this property, his family, this life. He stood up and found himself staring into a cabinet at a square wrapped in black silk. Blinking the dryness from his eyes made his head hurt worse. His fingers ran across the silk and undraped it, revealing the binding of the book. Then, before he could stop them, his hands opened to the page of the figure he'd never wanted to see again.

The crude woodblock picture of the figure wasn't blacked out in his copy, nor was the text beneath it, just a few lines explaining who it was, what it did, and what it would offer. Panic leapt through his body, knocking the wind out of him. His clenched jaw shot another wave of pain up his neck and into his head. He felt for the locus of the headache, rubbed it, and felt something less like a bump and more like a growing horn. The darkness of the shed folded around him like hateful origami.

Hakim struggled to control his breath and willed himself to shut the book. Mercifully, his hand obeyed, and the book dropped to the ground. Hakim thought to flee, to tear out of the workshop and find Nick and beat him to death for showing up, to wake his wife and tell her everything. She'd know what to do, how to save him now, the same way she'd always known how to save him, but then he stopped and tried the lighter again. To his surprise, it worked, and he picked up the book, opened it to the page, and held the flame to it.

The paper blazed and the book caught. Hakim dropped it on the floor and listened to the snakeskin cover crackle as the fire licked it. He kicked the book into the center of the room, watched it burn on the bare concrete. The fire intensified as it consumed more of the paper, and he couldn't help but see the building that night as they'd fled. When it died down a bit, he kicked the remaining unburned parts into a pile, the final fuel jumping with the hot light. When he was sure that nothing of the spirit list remained, he swept the ashes into a tidy pile and left the shed. He walked to the far end of his property, to the liminal edge marked by the fence, and threw the charred remnants towards the north.

He then took his clothes off outside, meditated, and returned to the house. He took an ibuprofen for his headache and tried not to keep touching the bump on his head, then crawled quietly into bed next to his sleeping wife.

When his head hit the Egyptian cotton pillow case, the top of his skull throbbed, radiating fibers of ache down into his back. When he tried to sit up and go to the medicine cabinet for more pills, he couldn't. He looked sideways to his sleeping wife and was trying to reach out to her, to wake her up for help, when the room went dark with the same inky black he had seen twice now; the first time outside the circle, then in his wizard workshop a few hours ago.

A rush of sharp discomfort cascaded down the front of his forehead and made his jaw clench. The pain panicked his body, and Hakim grabbed for the sheets, slapped around, hoping the movement would wake his wife. The skin of his neck tightened as he was lifted from his scruff like a puppy. The cone rising from the top of his head rubbed against the headboard, his face pulling backwards tighter and harder. He had the image of something sucking on the back of his head; he tried to scream, but the stretched skin held his mouth open like a vise.

With a muffled sound like a cotton shirt tearing, he was drawn backwards and up with another painful yank. He was looking down at his body, watching his hands clawing for anything they could grip. His taut skin, released now, had been stretched like taffy. It lay atop his shoulders in brown folds and, underneath, through a flap in the slackening skin, his eyes were wild in their sockets. He thought of meatballs hidden under twisting strands of nightmare spaghetti.

A tunnel was closing around him. Through the darkening orifice, he searched for the blood that was surely spraying the walls, soaking Danta, waking her. Any moment now, she would be up, she would see what was happening, she would reach for him.

The rest of Hakim's body, from the collarbones down, was desiccating. His wife, sleeping soundly next to a mummifying corpse, snored peacefully. His hands reached for the round walls of the closing tunnel, desperate to pull himself back through. He tensed his core to propel himself; nothing happened. The anger and helplessness brought him to shouting, and then screaming, a high-pitched sound so desperate and so feral that he was shocked to hear it, stupidly fearful that it would wake his daughters. But maybe if he woke them, they would come running in, see what was happening, and wake Danta. So he shrieked, he screamed, he begged and cried and screamed.

Danta only rolled over, her body stilling in the onset of deeper sleep.

What would happen when she woke up, rolled over and put her warm, slumber-heavy hands across his ribs, wondered why his skin felt like that, so wrinkled and dry? What would happen when his daughters bounced into his room and jumped on him? He thought of Flor, of seeing her, how long he'd thought about it, how many days and nights he'd lost to horrific visions. His sweet babies, seeing him like that, how long would they have to live with it? He couldn't help them now, he wouldn't be able to reach through and help them in any way.

Not where he was going.

"I didn't say anything to anyone!" he shouted. "I never said your name! I never said any—!" and then, the tunnel closed.

NINE

Nick found himself running through a house. A woman was yelling, and he was here to save her. He wound through hallways painted a soft, fuzzy white, throwing open doors and trying to find her. Every door led to a hallway full of more twists, more doors, more soft white. When he heard a door slam somewhere behind him, he grew frantic and found himself suddenly unable to grip the door handles to turn them. He was being chased now, footprints hard against the carpet, loud against the silence of the cyclopean residence, then behind him a bald man with his arm raised above his head, hand clutching something large and blunt and Nick suddenly awoke, sitting upright and clutching the off-colored motel sheets around him.

Instincts developed as a nightmare—ridden child kept his legs moving, getting under him, ready to leap in self-defense. His waking eyes fed the shapes of his surroundings to his brain. The motel room formed around him, grimy succor. A knock against a door down the hall sounded again, followed by a woman's voice, irritated and impatient, demanding to be let in. It wasn't his room, the sound was too far away. He snuck an arm out of the covers and grabbed the clock, turning the bright red numbers toward him. 1:15. He threw the clock away from him and groped for the light, switching it on and coming down from the adrenaline in the glow of a dusty lampshade.

He thought about Hakim, wondered if he should call him. Wondered if that's what cops do in certain situations. Had a cop ever seen something and bugged so hard that he had to go back and see? Had to pull certain favors to get into a cell at two in the morning, see the perpetrator? Had to use his worldly powers to get a victim's number and call and ask if they'd slept poorly tonight, too?

Resigned to wakefulness, Nick got out of the bed. His lower back was sore from so much sitting in the car, and he paced the small room, finding that the more time that passed between him and the nightmare, the more its power and influence waned. A couple of swigs of the flask emptied it, and eventually he stretched back out onto the bed and sighed.

Desperate to be brain-dead for a few merciful hours, Nick grabbed the remote from the nightstand and pointed it at the old TV on its old stand, thumbing the power button. Nothing happened. He hit it again and again and again, the fatigue sweeping over him and unfocusing his eyes. Light from the bedside lamp reflected off the screen, his silhouette with an arm raised towards the TV, pointing accusingly.

Then the black screen twisted between fuzz and clarity, and Flor was there, reaching for him, eyes full of love and passion and desire until her face changed, twisted in rictus. Then, she was pulled backwards, and he watched her growing smaller and smaller, requisitioned. Nick hurtled from the bed and onto the aged shag carpet, trying to reach through and grab her, his fingers thumping and bending backwards against the solid TV screen. She got smaller and smaller, and then a mouth appeared, bright red and pink and yellow against the black, and swallowed her like a fly.

He knew there was no sleeping after that. Nick's hand hit the power knob on the unit, and the TV lit up, hellish vision interrupted by a violently blue screen. He flipped through the channels for a long time, trying to find her, cathode ray tubes burning his irises as he searched every pixel of the screen for any sign of her, reluctantly stopping on a cop show deep into a late night marathon.

In one of the episodes, two detectives had gone to a house and played "good cop, bad cop." Nick was struck by the formality of the good cop; the politeness, the way he shook the woman's hand, the way he laid a trail of honey while the other cop followed with vinegar.

The motel room was bluing with the dawn when the cop show marathon was replaced by an infomercial for a Christian-based casket manufacturer. A man with two and half-chins, an ill-fitting white Oxford, and sweat-stained armpits assured Nick that Jesus had made a room for him and that they could provide the bed. Nick hit the power button on the remote and the unit, but neither worked: the man on the television kept displaying color and trim options for your custom eternal rest.

After a quick shower, Nick left the room, the TV still blaring.

TEN

The neighborhood was spare, five houses perched on the long stretch of street. Halfway down was an old Victorian, painted in blacks and purples, ironwork spider webs, and subtle goth décor spread about the metal and woodwork. He stopped his car in front of that one. There was only one neighbor close enough to see from the front porch where Nick stood, and its house was obstructed by a shoddy landscaping job, unruly-limbed bushes arching like arthritic hands and surely just as brittle, stretched at such angles it looked like the next wind would entirely uproot them.

There was no button indicating a doorbell, just an antique-looking dragon's head with a ring in its mouth, heavy and cold to the touch when Nick lifted it. Mid-swing, the door opened, the ornate brass thumping and clattering against a metal plate on the rebound. A gorgeous woman with pale skin, black hair, and cleavage thrusting out through the low cut of her dress stood in the doorway. She stared at Nick with a blank expression on her face and offered no greeting.

He forced his eyes back to her face and extended his hand. "Nick Kyle, private private investigator," he said, finally happy with how it sounded. After a long pause, he lowered his hand, "I'm looking for Jacqueline Crawford." The woman said nothing. "Is Jackie home?"

Again, the woman was silent, and over her shoulder appeared another woman, identical down to the dress.

He had a feeling she wouldn't tell him the answer, but he asked anyway. "Is she available?"

The woman shut the door. Frustration from the lack of sleep and dead ends of the last few days sent heat up his face before he remembered the politeness of the cops in the show, how the people being questioned would open up with a little patience and a composed tone of voice.

He knocked again, trying to be gentle, but the weight of the door serpent sounded with a deep, loud thump. "Do you know when she'll be back?" No answer. "Can you please tell me a good way to reach her?"

After a long moment, he stepped off the porch and backed up further into the yard to try and catch any movement in the windows. He saw none, and then looked down at the file folder he'd remembered to bring from the car this time, studying Jacqueline's picture again: a headshot from a metaphysical zine that listed her as a Wiccan priestess along with a host of other lofty titles that sounded like they were from Dungeons and Dragons.

It hadn't been Jacqueline who had answered the door. The woman in the picture was more plain, not nearly as voluptuous.

Nothing on the block had moved, no bird calls or sounds of traffic. On his way to the car, he noticed the strange angle of the thistle growing from cracks in the asphalt. He glanced at the house next door, looking again at the ponderous leaning of the hedge. A scan around him showed the same canted pattern in the entirety of the street's flora; all of it leaned perceptibly away from Jacqueline's. To Nick, it looked like the whole neighborhood was straining to flee.

Nick became acutely aware of his loitering and the sweat of his hands. He shut his car door quickly, ears ringing from the slam, and drove away without looking for the next address.

ELEVEN

Nick had swung the big brown sedan onto the exit ramp and turned right at the stop sign. Two lanes twisted themselves down miles of valley, tightly enclosed by dense pine and aspen. Houses were scattered as if cast by an unconcerned hand: a Swiss-style chalet, lots of log cabins, scatters of Pueblo Revival. Nick kept having to correct the car as his eyes flitted back and forth between the properties and the snaking road.

Around one of the bends, a black SUV perched at the end of a long driveway. Nick took his foot off the gas to curb his speed and passed the SUV, looking in his rearview to see if it was a cop about to pursue him. He saw two men, all in black, one looking at him and one on a radio. Then he was over another humped curve, and the SUV disappeared from his mirror.

Had he been speeding? He was driving erratically, kept swerving back to his side of the road, distracted by the houses. His car rose again on a slight incline and, at the apex, Nick flicked his eyes up to see the SUV behind him, and gaining.

The road ahead of him descended towards the driveway of a white pine McMansion, then curved sharply in front of the home's long driveway. He jammed the wheel to make the turn. The back of his car was faster than the front, and the sedan screeched sideways on the road, coming to a stop across both lanes. The SUV crested the hill, and Nick got a look now, enough to convince himself that this wasn't law enforcement, but definitely following him.

Nick found the lane again and barreled straight ahead, seeing that he was starting to climb a mountain, switchbacks as far up as he could see. The road came to a hairpin turn, and he slowed too much but turned enough, tires screeching. The car made it without spinning, the leather of the steering wheel wet and slippery under his hands, squawking and squelching in protest at his grip.

There could be a million reasons that SUV was behind him. Maybe it wasn't after him. This was a two-lane road; they could be headed up the mountain, too; there was only way to go. Behind him, a flash of black metal as the SUV rounded a corner.

Were they pointing at him?

Have to get more road underneath me, Nick thought. He remembered a movie he'd seen where someone was being followed, so they pulled off the road and hid behind a group of trees and a city limit sign. The pursuers had raced passed the hiding spot in all their heat, and the good guys were able to get the upper hand.

Nick had no better idea, so he began looking for any place to pull off the road. Multiple yellow signs showed traffic glyphs indicating sharp precipices on the side of the road and warnings not to pull off.

This is ridiculous, I'm getting paranoid, he thought. He waited for that to sink in, expecting relief, but only got a crawling apprehension down his spine.

Switchback after switchback, Nick's car climbed. The higher he got, the closer the trees hugged to themselves, blue shadows congealing on the road as the sun sank. In the rearview, the SUV. Still no place to pull off.

The road flattened, and Nick accelerated, then the trees opened up and a small town's buildings materialized. He wheeled the car into the first parking lot he saw, a gas station, braking to a hard stop at the pump, rear bumper to the road. Nick sat very still in the car, shoulders hunched to his ears and barely breathing as he stared out the rearview mirror. No cars coming. No lights coming.

Then, a pounding on his door.

Nick jumped, his whole body turning in the seat. Out his window, a man with a close-cut black beard and a grimy safety orange beanie on his head smiled at him. His mouth was moving, but Nick couldn't hear anything over the thump of his heart.

The man held up a gas pump handle in demonstration.

"Yeah, yeah, please," Nick said and started to roll down the window, feeling the chill mountain air spill into the humidity of the cabin. The SUV passed by behind him, the guy in the passenger seat staring deadpan at Nick's car like a sun-glassed basilisk.

Nick didn't want to turn his head, afraid the motion would trigger the predator, so only his eyes followed the SUV as it continued down the road and disappeared.

He jumped at the sound of the thumps and whoosh of gas rushing into his tank, and the man was at his window again. He had an accent that Nick couldn't recognize. Nordic? A flash of Flor's face in the winter cabin they had rented in Bergen. Sadness then, knowing a trip like that would never happen again.

"You ok, Mister?"

"Yeah, that road is kind of curvy. Couple of those sneak up on you," Nick said, expecting to see the SUV come from the other direction, the driver beaming daggers at him.

"You should see it in winter. What I miss in revenue from the gasoline on account of no one driving through, I make up with hauling cars back up the ravines."

Still no movement in the reflection. Nick's breathing slowed. "I'm surprised people are still alive to haul back up. That's a hell of a drop."

"Oh, they're not alive most of the time, just can't leave cars hanging off cliffs on the side of a mountain. Bad for business when people driving on the interstate look up into scenic mountain beauty covered in crashed cars. That be cash or card?"

"Cash," Nick said.

"Much obliged," the man said, then Nick heard the clicks and thumps of the gas hose being pulled out and the fuel door being shut. Nick handed the man a folded bill, watched as the man stuffed the bill into a front pocket of his overalls without looking at the denomination.

"You mind if I sit here a second and look over these directions?"

"Take your time, Mister."

Nick looked over the directions, tried to memorize the route through the small mountain town to Jared's address. The map was unsteady and dampening where he held the edges, so he put it down and focused on trying to figure out what the hell just happened. He didn't want to look any more out of the ordinary than he already did, so, on the pretense of having gotten himself together, he started the car.

"Safe travels, Mister," came the brogued voice from the parking lot.

Nick put the car in reverse but depressed the brake, hunching down and shouting out the window, "Say, did you see that black SUV that came up the road behind me? Do you know them? They locals?"

He saw the bearded man turn and regard him for a second and then light a cigarette. "Those boys that were following you? Nah, Mister, never seen 'em before."

TWELVE

Nick took the unfamiliar mountain roads carefully, loose rocks kicking under his tires as the asphalt turned to dirt. He found the turn he was looking for, sudden headlights blinding him in the middle of the hard angle. Nick took the turn wider to avoid a head-on collision, and when the car roared past him, he scanned his mirrors. The brilliance had left his vision a green flash, and his adjusting eyes only saw the trail of illuminated brake lights as the car took the corner.

Nick drove the dead-end street slowly, searching for any conspicuous address markings on the houses. He found a mailbox with the right number on it, then parked, facing downhill for an easier exit.

The folder on his lap said "Jared Knight," with no accompanying picture. This was the only person he couldn't get much information for, but the address matched.

Red lights ahead of him lit the cabin of his car. Nick's eyes moved before his head followed; turning right at the stop sign was a black SUV, its headlights off. It went fast around the corner, fishtailing slightly.

Attempting to remain calm, he triple-checked the address. *Lots of people drive SUVs,* he thought, *especially up here where who knows how bad the winter gets,* and he forced himself out of the car..

The house was below the grade of the street, down a steep driveway a short distance from where he was parked, and up a set of wooden stairs leading up to a deck. From here, the house wasn't much to look at — moldy cedar paneling and roof tiles peeling up like rotten toenails. Over the railing was a large patch of hemlock standing upright.

Flor loved poison plants. More than one of their hikes together had been interrupted by her stopping to coo at a deadly mushroom as if it were a cute puppy. No matter how innocuous-looking a plant or flower appeared, Flor could — and did — explain how it would kill you, and how quickly. She was never sadistic about this, though, as she'd then add in the next breath how, at lower doses, the same plant would heal you. "That liminal space," she would say, giggling with that deep laugh and covering her radiant smile with a bunched strand of hair.

Nick glowed inside, remembering her, imagining what she might have said about this deadly stand of hemlock swaying in the swelling night with no wind or breeze. The uncanny movement made him shudder, the warm memory fading into cold heartache and even colder apprehension: maybe they'd poisoned her? And worse: with a plant she'd introduced them to, taking advantage of her openhearted passion and generosity, tricking her into sharing insight and then murdering her with it.

He turned from the dancing stalks and tried to find the doorbell. Out of the corner of his eye, the leaves of the plants shimmied in the still air, and he hastily knocked on the door. He heard footsteps within, the sound of another door opening, and then the footsteps got closer. Through the broken screen window of the door, he could see what looked like an old hippy approaching, and Nick's heart dropped, embarrassed that he was bothering this old man.

The hippy opened the door, which flapped around with a twang uncharacteristic of wood, a face round with harmlessness peering out. "Yes?"

"My name is Nick Kyle, I'm looking for Jared Knight," Nick mumbled, disheartened.

"Can I help you?" the man said. He was somewhere in middle age, fit, with long, silver hair tied back into a ponytail and a trimmed beard. He wore harem pants, a plain black shirt with some grey spots scattered over the front. There was no big silver pentagram around his neck, nor a sinister, pointed goatee. Just some old hippy in the mountains.

"Are you Jared Knight?"

"Usually," the man said. Nick's heart leapt into his throat. Despite the adrenaline rush, Nick suddenly felt very tired and worn.

"Nick Kyle, private private investigator," Nick said, holding his hand out, but keeping his elbow slightly cocked against his side to prevent Jared from seeing it trembling.

They shook hands and stood in an awkward pause before Jared cocked an eye at Nick in an attempt to coax the situation forward.

"Oh, uh, I came to ask you some questions about Horace 'Daathioz' Pantalione."

"Is this about him being dead?"

"I found — I mean, yes. I have reason to believe he might be dead, yes." A breeze of cold air whipped up, swirling around them. "Were you somehow aware of his death?" His words caught mid-sentence, stolen by the ice-edged breeze. Nick turned his head out of the wind, opening his mouth to catch his breath. He felt the collar of his thin shirt flapping. The wind gusted again, and the hemlock stood dead still. Goosebumps crawled up Nick's arms.

"Are you a cop?"

"No, I'm not a cop, I'm a priv— "

"Good, come in then. I have a feeling I know what you're looking for."

THIRTEEN

"Can I get you some coffee or a drink, man?" Jared asked, opening a cabinet. "Been working on my mint julep lately."

"Coffee is fine." The kitchen was a little dirty, its walls lined with yellow pine cabinets and grungy white appliances. Nick's eyes followed the dark tiled floor to a large cased opening that led from the kitchen into a sizable living room with a much higher ceiling. From his place at the bar, Nick could see that the center of the living room was sunken a few feet into the ground and filled with cushions and a perfectly fitted, huge red leather couch.

"Want a little zip in it?" Jared shook a vodka bottle, the clear liquid sloshing around.

"Just black, thank you. I just have a few questions; don't wanna take up too much of your time tonight. I'd like to get down the mountain before it gets too dark." While the coffee percolated and Jared mixed a drink for himself, Nick wandered to the threshold and peered in.

The wall to the left was one big projection screen bordered by two tall cabinets that held a large selection of movies. Two of the other walls of the room were completely covered with full bookshelves, atop which even more books were stacked haphazardly, punctuated by weird statues. Nick recognized Horus and Osiris, but many more were pieces he couldn't place, ithyphallic and strange.

"Hot coffee for the traveler," Jared said, offering Nick the mug. On his middle finger, Jared wore a golden ring. Nick tried not to stare, instead turning to look up at the tall ceiling, expecting to see herbs hanging but finding instead only dirty skylights. "So, what's up, man? I can tell you're not a cop."

Nick hid the search for his next remark behind a long sip of coffee. "I've been hired by a private group to investigate some disappearances."

"A private group, huh? To investigate the death of a speed freak in a tent city?"

"How did you know Horace?"

"How did *you* know Daathioz?" Jared shot back, turning to a drawer by the sink. He opened it and brought out a small, jeweled dagger. Something about the glint of it made Nick's coffee stop at his lip. Nick's eyes watched Jared, then judged his distance from the front door.

"Who are you?" Jared asked, calmer, putting the dagger into his drink, stirring, then tossing the dagger into the sink and taking a sip. "More sugar. Hang on, man," and Jared disappeared into the small hallway.

Nick watched him, then glanced over to the bookshelves. The first book his eye went to was a copy of the one he was currently shuttling around. *Of all the books on all the shelves*, he thought.

When Jared didn't immediately reappear, Nick got up and crossed to it. If Jared came out of the hallway holding a gun, maybe the distance would be enough. Instead, Jared reappeared with a brown, plastic container. He opened it and spooned a small lump of something that Nick thought looked like sand into his cup.

"I like to read," Jared said, noting Nick's attention on the book. He then motioned to two armchairs, both simply carved and covered in cushions of lavender paisley. They sat and sipped their drinks in silence until a flurry of static noise and tinny voices shouted across the room from somewhere in the kitchen — a police scanner. Nick couldn't understand what was said.

"How did you know Horace?" Nick asked again. Jared looked at him for a long time in the same searching way Hakim had. Nick squirmed in his chair and hoped Jared thought he was just settling in.

"Daathioz and I were involved in a — fraternal organization, let's say."

"I thought women were involved?" By the way Jared looked at him, Nick knew he had given up too much, too soon."It's kind of like Spanish, man; anytime you introduce one male into the equation, it changes the definite article. Five hundred sisters, one brother, it's a fraternal organization. One of those holdover things from a long ago time. Besides, the magic was the point. Or was supposed to be the point, anyway."

"How long were you involved?" Nick asked, sipping his coffee. Something in the air of the room gave, and Jared's reluctance went with it.

"Twenty years. The last fifteen, I was really hardcore about it. I spent a lot of free time doing everything I could to help people attain, man. I'd ignore everyone — friends, family — and just spend my entire weekends memorizing lines for initiation rituals and shit."

"Sounds like you're a little bitter."

"I *was* bitter, man, but the bottom line is I'm doing magick and they're not, and look where I am," Jared stopped and held his hands up, motioning around the room. "And look where they are."

"Dead."

"Only one of them, man. And he was really working, say what you want about his personal consumption habits."

"When was the last time you saw him?"

"Have you been watching cop shows or something? Are you asking me if I killed Daathioz? And if you have his book, wouldn't that make you a likely suspect?"

Nick threw out that line of questioning; the alacrity with which Jared had picked it up alarmed him. How did Jared know he had the book? He thought to tell him about Brock and the tour busses but decided to hold that card.

"Why do you have his book, man?"

Nick opened his briefcase, flipped past the folder on Jared quickly, hoping he didn't see his name in large letters on the side of the envelope. He tossed the book gently onto the small side table between them, then stood and slid Jared's copy off the shelf.

"Don't open that," Jared said.

"It looks quite well-thumbed."

"Don't open it. Put it back and ask me your next question."

Nick hesitated. The itch to open it up to the page and see — and then Jared was suddenly at his side, grabbing it and pulling it swiftly away. He spilled some of his drink but ignored it, shelved the book carefully, and only then wiped the dripping excess off his shirt. When he sat back down, he eyed Nick's copy and reached for it. Nick let him, watched him open it and then spot the big black redaction.

"That's why he called," Jared said, almost to himself. He swished his glass, the ice tinkling. "I'm gonna get another. More coffee?"

"Please. He called you?" Nick asked, projecting his voice so that Jared would catch it as he crossed the room. That's when he did it. If pressed, he wouldn't have been able to explain why or how, but something moved through him and he switched the books. He didn't have time to thumb through and see if Jared's copy was marked out. He simply grabbed Daathioz's copy from the table and Jared's from the bookshelf and swapped their places.

"He asked me if I still had my copy. The occult book resale market is basically a money tree. So many boutique publishers print something once and never make more copies. Books from even ten years ago have tripled in value. You find a couple copies of certain books — this one included," Jared said, "and you can make a couple thousands in days. Maybe even five figures. You just gotta know who to take it to. Especially because this one never really made it to press."

"What do you mean it never made it to press? There are other copies of it that I've seen. "

The radio squawked again.

"I have a homegirl who got on the board of the publisher, guided them gently away from the idea."

"Jacqueline Crawford?"

Jared sipped his drink, and Nick watched him calculate.

"Yeah, Jacqueline Crawford," Jared said. Nick felt a rise, a positive pulse, his weariness fleeing.

"How'd she do that?"

"I'm sure from the outside this looks like a big world, but it's a small scene. You make a little splash, hell, a little ripple, and people know your name. Soon you start getting invited to things, meeting more people — you do things and things happen, man."

"So this one didn't get republished?"

"It didn't even get published. She only sent a couple out."

"How many copies are extant?" Nick said, pleased with the technical word that had just come to him.

"Where did you see other copies?"

"And Daathioz was trying to buy yours?" Nick said, side-stepping Jared's question.

"More like *take* it, man. He wasn't exactly in a buying position."

"And why do you think he was trying to take it?"

"Well, I thought he was gonna sell it. But now that I see this copy, and you here, and him dead—" The radio squawked again, and Jared cocked his ear to listen.

"Is that a scanner?"

"It's kind of like a scanner, but for the whole town. The winter can get grim. We get stuck up here all the time, so this helps us communicate, send news back and forth. Serves kinda like a town crier. People who aren't from around here come up, thinking they can get some pretty winter pictures to frame and sell at their local coffee shops or whatever, and they drive off the road all the time, so old Bjorn — the guy at the little gas station on your way into town — he owns a tow truck and likes to dispatch. Makes him feel useful, I guess. Someone drives off the road, Bjorn tells the whole town. Sounds like someone may have gone off. Those numbers — arbitrary, picked by Bjorn based on his former wife's birthday — are what he uses when he's at the scene with his tow truck."

"Jacqueline Crawford," Nick said, trying to bring the conversation back around.

"You looking for her, too?"

"I am, actually. Was at her house today, no one home except—"

"She left right before you came in. She came up to buy some weed and chat. We like to get together sometimes."

Nick stopped, remembering the SUV following the car that had nearly blinded him. When Flor's parents had hired him to find her, they hoped that someone with some skin in the game would actually give a shit and look for her, knowing they'd been lovers. Would they have hired someone else? Someone more professional? Someone to follow him? His grip around the coffee tightened.

"How did you get our names?" Jared asked.

"Did you see a black SUV driving around here? Before she left?" Nick said, watching Jared tense.

"No, I didn't."

The radio squawked again. Nick recognized the accented voice from the gas station and listened a bit closer.

"We're pulling it up now, and it looks like just a woman," the radio said. Nick's stomach dropped, and he felt himself go pale. Jared saw Nick's face and bolted for the door, dropping his glass into the sink and grabbing keys off a hook with practiced speed. Nick followed him out into the clammy night, Jared already unlocking the door of his Jeep.

FOURTEEN

Jackie pulled into the gas station with a pain in the middle of her chest. She wrote it off to the high altitude, a couple of joints with Jared, the crying she'd done over Daathioz and Brock, and probably Hakim, too. Though that one hadn't been confirmed, she *knew*.

I should probably drink some water, she thought, grabbing a metal bottle from the cup holder. She put it to her lips and raised her chin to drink. Her eyes caught something in the rearview mirror: a black SUV pulled in behind her and stopped. Inside it, two guys in mirrored sunglasses, despite the night's arrival. They turned off their headlights, neither of them moving to get out of the car.

She put the bottle back in the cup holder. Consciously minimizing her movements so as not to telegraph her actions, she opened her purse in the passenger seat, pushed the glass jar full of weed and mushrooms deeper in, and covered it with her notebook, wallet, and compacts. When she looked again, the two men were staring directly at her.

A voice made her jump. "Evening, ma'am." She looked out her window at a man gesturing at the gas nozzle in his hand. He pointed at it, lifted an eyebrow, and then shrugged to mime the question.

She opened the door and stepped out of the car, putting her back to the stares.

"Oh, no bother, ma'am, this is a full-service station. Can I get you to pop your gas cap for me?" the man said in a heavily-accented voice. Jackie leaned back into her car and pushed on the panel for the gas tank. It flopped open limply, and she tried very hard not to look back as she wedged her dark lacquered nails carefully into the small crack of the gas door and opened the panel. She then stepped aside and watched the man start the pump.

His job done, the attendant walked towards the SUV. "Can I help you, fellas?" They didn't reply, only continued to stare at Jackie.

Jackie felt the gas station attendants' attention return to her. She met his eyes, hoping with a stern, unflinching look to mutualize the weirdness of the people in that car. She coughed, and it hurt.

The gas pump stopped, and the attendant closed the door and returned the nozzle to its holder with practiced ease. He gave her the total, then walked back towards the SUV. She stepped into her car, wincing at the muscle spasm, and fished in her wallet for the cash. Her rear-view mirror showed the driver's attention on the attendant, but the passenger was still focused on her.

When the attendant shuffled back, she handed him the bill. He took it and smiled politely. "Drive safe, ma'am." She held his gaze a second, but his eyes gave nothing away.

She left the gas station as quickly as she could.

As the town disappeared behind her into the thick forest, Jackie fished a cough drop from her purse. She couldn't unwrap the wrinkly paper with just one hand — it had long ago fused to the ancient lozenge. She slowed down her car enough to open it with both hands, just before the switchbacks started.

Around the first sharp curve, she saw the headlights of the SUV behind her. "Shit," she said, and then coughed again, shooting another sharp pain through her chest.

Unconsciously, her hand slipped into her purse again to make sure the jar Jared had given her was still there. She'd taken this turn a bit too fast, though, and her tires made a noise. She slowed down for the next, and found herself thinking about Jared — and that night.

She'd picked up Daathioz at his apartment early. Jackie had always liked being the first one to the party, so they'd left an hour before Daathioz had wanted to. They'd somehow gotten lost, and when Jackie finally stomped her medium height, medium build, extra large serving of Goth into the strange building, she was nearly in tears.

"I am so sorry we're so late, the directions weren't exactly clear, and we drove past these trees five times. They didn't look — like they could have a building between them," Jacqueline said. Hakim gave her a big hug. He was her occult big bro — they'd come up together and had recently started co-teaching some classes. His affection was like a sedative, and she felt her jangling nerves calm until he let go and she got a good look at the place.

The dusk was settling, and the failing sunlight wouldn't catch on the walls of the building. Her composure faltered again, and this time, she wasn't sure that it was all up to her tardiness.

Then they stepped in, Daathioz behind her. She'd almost forgotten that he was there.

"Hey, Horace," Jared said.

"Use my real name, please," the skinny man said.

"Horace is your real name. Can you bring that box in here? Please?" Brocken said, pointing.

"Not until you address me by my real name," Horace said, planting himself.

"Daathioz, please set the box here," Jared said. Horace complied.

"What the fuck is a Daathioz, anyway?" Brocken said.

"A name given to me by the great spirit of the grimoire I just successfully completed working," Daathioz said.

"Oh gods, I'm hungry," Hakim said from the door.

"Someone forgot their apple cider vinegar water, huh?" said Jackie.

"Hey, Jacque," said Jared. "You got those tapers?"

Jackie reached into a black velvet sack and pulled out some thick candles, then two more, then another two, and handed them to Jared.

Brocken was helping Mike haul boxes out of the room now. "Set this by the other stuff," Brocken said.

"You set this by the other stuff, dude. I'm fucking hungry," Mike said, and sat down grumpily.

"We're all hungry, Lambchops. Move these empty boxes out of the room," Brock said, moving his long hair back behind his ears and out of the way.

"Well, she certainly came back with a set-up," Jackie said, taking a minute to let her vision fill with the sight. The room, almost set, glittered with shining metal.

"Man, I'll say. And all completely to the book," said Jared. He put his arm around her, and she returned the gesture. They stood there, looking at the temple equipment as a weird silence fell upon the throng.

"You guys really think this is going to work?" asked Mike, slumped in a corner and rubbing his head.

"Who even are you?" Jackie addressed him, although she was secretly glad that he'd cut through the pause.

"This is Mike, the extra," said Jared.

"Flor was in my coven for a while and, at the risk of sounding overconfident, and to spare you several very interesting stories, yes," said Daathioz, struggling past them with another box.

Mike shrugged. "You guys live in shitty apartments — how did you afford all this?"

"Oh, Flor is rich," Daathioz said, almost as an afterthought. He set the box down, and Jackie heard a dull thud where there should have been resonance. She felt the hair on her arms rise.

Hakim was about to come in and begin the preliminaries, but before she stepped out, Jackie overlooked it one last time and felt the frisson again. She had never been in a setup quite like this: a table in the north — The Altar, around it the bronze candlesticks, and before it a huge black carpet. Two cubed tables in the middle for the operating magician's weapons and book. *It sure looks like it might work*, she thought, then turned and left the room.

And it had worked. The week after the ritual, she'd gotten a letter. Her uncle had died, and she was listed in the will. He had no other heirs, and the money was enough to net fifty thousand just in annual interest. She lived comfortably off that, bought her house and property. That first year had been one of indolence and recreation, but then she needed something to do. So, she bought the office building, started a store, rented out the other sections. She'd worked hard to get that little witchy shop going, and Jackie felt blessed and enchanted. Everything always lined up perfectly, from the permits to the contractors to the tenets. She'd never gone into the red, and her classes and workshops were always full.

But some nights, lying awake in the throes of an insomnia that nothing had ever touched — and she'd tried everything — Jackie thought of Flor in fine detail, with nearly total recall, down to the smudged eyeliner when the dagger plunged in, thick ennui smothered in violent rapture.

Flor had not shown an inch of hesitation before, but, lying there nearly pinned to the table, Jackie had seen the façade fall, for just a split second, until the fear dropped like rose petals, revealing the bud of ecstasy. On those bad nights, Jackie would watch it happen, and it would replay in her head, over and over and over until the sun finally released her.

But when she'd burned her copy of the book, the insomnia and nightmares had stopped. One night after hours of fitful tossing and turning, she got up and crossed the bedroom to a painting on the wall — a framed print of *The Accolade* by Edmund Leighton — and pulled it towards her. It opened like a door, and she keyed the combo for the safe hidden behind it. A woman's voice grunted in inquiry, and Jackie half-shut the safe before glancing back to the bed.

"Go back to sleep," Jackie said.

The woman lay back down, pulled the covers up, and the other woman in the bed draped her arm across the blanketed bundle. The room went silent with sleep, and Jackie pulled the book from the safe, swallowing involuntarily and opening right to the page, to the demon they'd summoned.

She swayed with a whole-body shiver, then shut the book. Without thinking, she'd walked into the backyard and, under the light of the moon, she burned the book in the gas barbecue, poking at the ashes and cinders to make sure it had been completely destroyed like the rest of them.

She should never have sent those copies out.

❦

Jackie negotiated another turn. It felt like the same turn as the last eight, and her chest pain was much worse. She was braking for a corner when the headlights were behind her, too bright in her eyes. Her breath caught, jagged pain like claws. She tried to inhale, but it hurt too badly, her sides in horrible stitches. She rubbed her ribs and felt her skin extending outwards at grotesque angles. She couldn't help it; she looked down. Her last thought before slamming against the side of the mountain was hooks. Hooks that would attach under her ribs and leave her to hang securely, like stored meat.

Her car ricocheted off the granite wall and was sent spinning and tumbling savagely into a ravine, landing nose down on a small outcropping. It stopped suddenly enough to break Jackie's neck with the torque, the back tires of the car coming to rest against the side of the mountain. Gravity pulled her broken body down in the seat. She could feel broken bones inside her chest, shards impaling her lungs and poking out her back, stapling her to the seat.

She couldn't have made a noise of any kind, yet her soul screamed as the force of her spirit being ejected from her body rent the quiet car like the sound of popping champagne.

A well of murk closed in around her, and she recognized three other voices from her past, heard them wailing through the black. The numinous inner light, spoken of by sages from time immemorial, that had minutes ago animated her body, recognized its new place of arrival. Finding itself in the company of desolation, Jackie's soul slumped, weeping.

FIFTEEN

J ackie got a call from Danta, Hakim's wife," Jared said. He turned the wheel again, and they were out of the neighborhood, racing through town. "Hakim is dead. Jackie knew Daathioz was dead, and she felt like Brocken was dead, too."

"What — wait, what do you mean she felt like Brocken was dead?"

"That's part of what she got, man," Jared said, but Nick had only heard part of that sentence, watching the gas station flying by. No one was outside, and the station's lights were off. The little town was eerily quiet, silence where Nick expected sirens and flashing reds and blues.

"You don't have police in town?"

"Nah, no one wants to do it. County Sheriffs are responsible, but they have to come up from the valley." Jared said. "We look out for each other, kind of anarchic up here. It's part of what I asked for."

Nick's skin crawled. If Hakim was dead, and Nick was right about Brock, and that radio news he had heard—

"What do you mean 'what you asked for?'"

"How much do you know about what happened?" Jared said, taking the first hairpin confidently.

"I know Flor went out there—" Nick said. Jared hit the brakes for the next turn, and Nick jerked forward against the seatbelt and then sideways as the Jeep careened around the corner.

"Flor?" Jared said.

"Floriana Sanchez-Gonzales."

"You said you were here about Horace. What do you know about Flor?" Jared slowed, putting the pieces together mid-corner. "Who hired you?"

Nick could see lights below them, the flashing colors of emergency strobes that conjoined on the granite walls of the mountain in sickly purples as they made their way up from the town at the base of the peak. "Her family," Nick said, his neck craning at the window, looking down, expecting a huge, dramatic scene.

"Bullshit, you were the boy she said she was tooling around with," Jared said. He accelerated down a straightaway and braked extra hard for the corner.

"Tooling around with?"

"Holy shit, you really don't know anything, do you?" The lights were up ahead now, two men standing outside a tow truck, orange lights revolving limply around the top. Jared slammed on the brakes, and the Jeep came to a halt close to the guardrail.

Then Jared was out and running up to the men. Nick's door was against the metal rail, so he had to shuffle over the center console and climb out the driver's side. He could see Jared and the Nordic guy talking, but he couldn't hear what they were saying over the metallic whine of the winch.

Nick was motion-sick and overwhelmed. He stopped halfway to the tow truck and stuck his head over the guardrail, yearning for fresh air. The sheer drop of the cliff below made him light-headed. He found himself on his knees, cold metal against his back, the spinning lights disorienting him. His eyes found Jared, the only solid object he could cling to, and the voices swam through.

"Can't tell if anyone's still in there, someone passing the gas station said they saw fresh tire tracks and a broken guardrail, thought I should check it out." Gears whined and metal sang of strain below them.

"That's her car," Jared said, leaning far over the edge. Nick swallowed hard and caught Jared's glance, but his eyes were vacant of the anchor Nick was desperate for. The winch pulled and pulled, sticking, metal scraping loudly.

Emergency services — an ambulance and a fire truck, two patrol cars — had arrived, and people clamored out of the vehicles just as the mangled car came over the rise, the tow truck rocking a bit as the car it hooked swung pendulously in the air.

They watched, all silent, as Bjorn got into the truck and edged it forward a bit, bringing the car up and over the road. He huffed back out and made his way to the panel of controls near the rear bumper. With a couple of flicks of his wrists, the car nose-dived, landing on its front bumper with crunches of plastic and broken glass. It balanced precariously for a split-second, and then crashed back to the ground, landing upright.

Getting a fire truck up that windy road had frustrated the firefighters, and with giant metal claws, they ripped into the car door with vigor. When they had it wrenched off, they took a step back. Two of the firefighters turned around and gagged.

Jared was standing still and quiet, staring into the cracked and spidered windshield, the first time tonight that Nick hadn't seen the man moving around like a perpetual motion machine. Jared moved cautiously around, looking in through the remnants of the passenger window.

A large silver pentagram around a mummified neck shone in the harsh floodlight of the rescue vehicles. Desiccated strands of dyed black hair almost reached to the top of black velvet clothes encasing a body dry as a husk. Nick thought of the mummies he'd seen in private tours of Egypt, thought of Flor, thought of the way she had worked herself and others into places that no one else could. The way he never would without her again, those moments gone.

The body in this car looked every bit as old as the best of those dead royalty, but it had probably been here for a few hours, tops. Jared choked back a sob. Nick felt his stomach bubble as his bowels threatened to loosen. Horror buzzed in the night air, nipping at everyone on the scene.

She was still belted in, her chest flayed outwards like a biology exhibit, and Nick thought suddenly of Horace's shriveled corpse. He choked back a retch. Jared, standing in front of Nick by the pulverized hood of the car, turned to him, ashen white. When Nick put his hand on Jared's shoulder, he felt it trembling.

The activity in front of them passed like a time-lapse of a bee's hive. The county sheriff sounded confused, didn't know what to do with the body, but the paramedics had agreed to transport the corpse to the Coroner's office in the nearby city. Extraction had begun then, and the gleaming white sheet of the gurney under the reflection of the moonlight strained Nick's eyes.

He vaguely remembered crawling over the center console again, Jared starting to drive.

"Should I be scared like this?" Nick said out loud, to no one. He felt the oppressive gravity of uphill hairpin mountain turns. Jared said nothing, driving quietly back to his house. When they were parked in the driveway, Jared looked over at Nick, who saw that the tears on his face had dried, the trembling had stopped.

"Who hired you?" Jared asked quietly.

"Her family, but — it's —" and then Nick's feelings detonated. "She was the love of my life, and she just disappeared. She just left. She was gone. She never said anything. She told me nothing, and she just left. And I miss her, and I just — I had to know. I have to know. So when her family approached me, I —"

"To Know, To Will, To Dare —" Jared started. He looked at Nick, anticipating. Nick just stared back at him, awkwardly, knowing he was being cued, clueless as to what. Then, in his head, like a rose being held over a furnace was Flor's voice, shouting, screaming. An image of her kitchen, stainless steel with one wooden plaque above the sink, the phrase engraved into it.

"To Keep Silent," Nick finished.

"Come inside, man."

SIXTEEN

The tall ponderosa pines around Jared's house scratched at the moonlight, rending it into thin strips that retreated suddenly in the headlights. Nick and Jared were on their way up the deck stairs, and both turned towards the source of the bright light; Jared put his right foot onto the landing and then slipped. His leg shot forward into an awkward front split, and his back knee went down, slamming into the edge of the wooden step.

Nick couldn't catch him in time, but offered him a hand and helped Jared sit down. Jared clutched his groin and groaned.

"What the hell did you slip on?" said a voice from the direction of the extinguished lights. The car door shut, and a man with short-cropped hair stood in the shadows. Another door opened and the light in the car re-illuminated as a woman got out of the front, and three people weaved ungracefully out of the back.

"Oh, shit, man, I forgot about the party," Jared said. He stood and limped to the door, opening it and flipping on the porch light. Closer now, Nick saw how attractive these people were. A blonde woman in a tight-fitting body suit stood next to the man, and three cute women were behind him, two of them carrying plastic grocery bags; all were dressed in various states of a Saturday night out. One twirled her hair as she looked at Nick.

"Hey, sorry we're late, there was an accident on the mountain, and traffic was blocked up for like two hours," said the man. Nick nauseated at the blithe referral to the accident. "Christian," the man said, sticking his hand out to Nick. "And this is Luna, on account of her white hair and the way she shines in the night," he said. Luna slapped his shoulder and giggled.

"Nick Kyle, private private investigator," Nick said, trying to turn on his act but hearing it droop instead as he flashed back to

Jackie's hollowed-out corpse. Though the girls smiled, the gap between these two situations was too big for Nick to cross, his body responding only with grief. At a loss, Nick turned and followed Jared inside. The air in the house was warm and stuffy, full of the miasma of anxiety they'd left in their wake.

"Hey, man, everything alright tonight?" Christian said, catching the mood in the air.

"Yeah, man. Who else is coming?" Jared said, but Nick heard no spirit in it.

Christian pulled out a bottle of wine. "Bunch of people, think I had it at more than ten last count. You got an opener for this?"

"In the drawer," Jared said. "You guys make yourselves at home. I gotta finish something up." Jared motioned Nick into the small hallway.

"Get you gentlemen a drink?" Christian called.

"Whiskey, neat," Nick said.

"I'll make a mint julep when I get back up here," Jared said. He walked down the small hallway, opened a door, and flipped on a light. It brightened a small office, neatly clean and homogenous in matching maple-colored furniture.

Nick took in what little detail was offered: a frame on the wall said that Jared had a doctoral degree in physics and some scattered trinkets implying a defense-contracting job. Jared sat down at the desk across from Nick. To defend himself from the sudden onset of the inarticulate, Jared picked up a Scottish Rite Freemasonry pen, and Nick watched his eyes grow distant while his fingers began to fidget.

Jared had always been fascinated by the occult and mathematics and had been given the pen when he joined the Masons at 18, and then got his PhD in math at 24. After a decade, the local old men's group had begun to stagnate, and Jared found some scabrous version of a Golden Dawn group. A member of that had then pointed him to another large magical organization. He immediately initiated in this bigger one, and that's where he'd met Jackie and Flor.

The troubles he had with that group were legion, and his mind raced passed the angst and bullshit of it and his subsequent expulsion. Some members — including Jackie — left in protest of his removal, and it had all gone quiet dramatically. Jared and the ones who left with him started a couple of little groups in that shadow, but none of them lasted. Jared remembered the time after his expulsion from that organization as a waveform; peaks of excitement and troughs of misery.

Friends had turned on him, but new forms of lifestyle had arrived. Flor had left a year before he was expelled and had just disappeared, until Jackie had called him one day, looking for some party favors. When she arrived for the pick up, Flor was with her, and even more radiant.

Flor didn't come from money. When she joined the Order, she couldn't even afford a tarot deck. Scholarships had kept her afloat, donations and generosity from other members paying most of her dues, with Flor occasionally making her own payments from a flotilla of part-time jobs. So, he was intrigued by her sweater — a cashmere with the word "Givenchy" unsubtly printed across the chest.

He asked her where she'd been, and over the next several hours and multiple pots of tea, Flor then unfolded wild stories of Europe: weird back alleyways in small Italian towns, hiking in Germany under stormy skies, tryst fun with trust funds. Jared couldn't believe any of it at first, and Jackie said she hadn't either until she saw Flor's suitcases filled with designer clothes and old books.

Flor had told them all this and more with absent emotion. Jared found himself wondering if she could have done what she'd said and returned more jaded than she'd been before. And then from a small leather backpack with the letters MCM printed all over it, she pulled out a book.

From Jared's extensive experience, he knew grimoires were common in the occult world. Pretty standard European Magick stuff. Monks, priests, mathematicians, philosophers, and kings used them, poring over spirit lists and chanting strangely in chalky circles by sooty candlelight. They were dispersed all over Europe, then beyond, translated and re-translated. Wealthy families collected them, sat on them, sold them to museums when their bloodlines and bank accounts ran dry.

But not all of the books were equal to others. Most of them had been changed a bit, or had blinds put in that required a certain level of magical proficiency in order to spot. Anyone with enough experience could find the cues, stitch them together, and make an attempt, hoping to see the sparks of result glimmer before their eyes.

But some of these books went unchanged, and though they became rarer and rarer, there were always rumors of their availability and potency. Lots of those books had been burnt on pyres, kindling for their sinful owners. Even Popes in proximity to these tomes were accused of necromancy and executed.

Flor had returned with just such a one. Jared was doubtful.

She'd been in a club in Monaco, she said, making eyes at a fit olive skin in a tight polo shirt when a drink came down the bar from him. She walked over, boldly American, and after only an hour of flirting over drinks, they left. After another bar and an expensive breakfast at sunrise, he brought her aboard his yacht, there to sail to Ibiza. After a frenzied, drunken roll and a nap in the gigantic master bedroom, they'd woken to a lunch of fresh fruit and honeyed salmon — Flor said she'd never forget the taste of that fish — and lain on the deck in the sun, sharing stories, finding themselves in a mutual appreciation for the occult. She'd laughed as she told Jared and Jackie about her embellished background of Spanish royalty. Jared remembered that laugh because it was the first and only display of happiness in the entirety of her visit and the last time he ever heard it from her.

The boy was some kind of count or duke or something, she couldn't understand the line. His family had a book that went back hundreds of years, he'd said. Did she want to see it?

He'd brought them out of the sun and into a gold-rimmed cabin, took an innocuous-looking book from a polished shelf of dark, rare wood, and started turning crisp, yellowed pages. She couldn't read the Latin, but he could and did. They sipped champagne as he went over the book with her, their bodies entwining on an overstuffed leather couch. She plied him with more bubbly, and as he got more drunk, his lips got looser.

With his family's permission, a small print run of this book was in the works, with a few changes they'd neglected to share with the publisher. But this was the real one. Only four copies of the original text were known: one in a private collection, one in a university in Munich, the other two destroyed in WW2 under fascist blitzkrieg. The private collection had been his grandfather's, and his grandfather's before that.

She's asked him what was so special about this one, and he'd told her. This was the only copy that worked. So people wouldn't hurt themselves, he'd explained. The one in Munich was wrong, had things omitted on purpose, a different set of incorrect details from those in the one to be printed by a boutique British publisher.

Then they'd landed and partied in Ibiza. The plan was a week, then sail back to meet his family. He was smitten, but Flor was over him by the third day. All she could think about was that book. One night, after a particularly long night of dancing and a tantric session that left him dead to rights, she stole it, slipped through the anonymous crowds on the island, boarded a plane with a ticket paid for in cash, and was now here on Jared's living-room floor, planning a ritual.

When she talked about what they were going to do, the ennui that hung around her like a noxious perfume lifted. Her eyes gleamed like a lioness about to jump on prey. "These magical lodges," she said, "they're old news. Old aeon of the new aeon." It was all about working groups, she'd explained. Anarchic Witch Cults. Ritual magick strike teams. One and done, and then the group disperses. No hierarchies, no grade levels. A small handful of people — honed magicians handpicked by themselves — meeting under the cover of darkness for a singular mission like an occult SWAT team. Jared had thrilled at the idea but was mystified by the militancy in her language. He agreed, though, right there. Jackie and Jared both knew a few people they could get to join.

And then, Flor had left back to Europe. The next time he saw her was the night in that strange building.

There was a knock on the door that interrupted the awkward silence and Jared's reverie. When he rose from his office chair, Jared's groin throbbed. Holding himself, he opened the door a crack. Christian offered the half-full glass of whiskey to Nick, who took it gratefully, took a sip, and relished the warmth that radiated down.

"Didn't know you had people over tonight," Nick said.

"Would you have not come, or something?" Jared tugged at his crotch, wincing as he nearly fell back into his chair.

"Well, I don't wanna keep you, but after what we saw tonight, I just—"

"Have some questions? Me, too."

"What happened to Flor?" Nick asked after stoking courage with another sip of whisky.

"Same thing that happened to Jackie. And Brocken, and Hakim," Jared said, letting that hang in the air to see if Nick picked it up.

"What happened to Hakim?" Nick asked, unable to hide his nervous gulp of whiskey. Jared tugged at his groin. "You ok ?"

"I was. I was having a good night until some asshole knocked on my door. Then I saw a good friend of mine hoisted from the abyss like a mummy, forgot I was hosting an orgy, and pulled a muscle in my groin. The combination of all this shit is giving me heartache and phantom limb pain in my cock, man. How do you know about any of this?"

Nick hesitated, but after tonight's events and the intimacy of what they'd both seen, he opened up. "Her family waited a year. Kept her loft downtown, didn't touch anything. The cops quit caring about some missing brown girl, nothing came up no matter how much her father hounded. And then they just got rid of everything. I couldn't — I still can't understand doing that after only a year, but I told them I agreed with their decision and volunteered to handle it. I'd have an estate sale, they could have what they wanted. Which wasn't much: stuffed teddy bear, some pictures, and keepsakes. I'd get rid of it all. Split the money."

Nick paused, his eyes misting. "But the way they just gave up looking for her — and I had to know. I couldn't sleep, I couldn't eat. I lost my job because all I did was sit there rifling through newspapers, going through the police reports over and over, going through our memories. So I rented a storage locker, took everything she owned there instead. I would go in when I could stomach it, look through everything, smelling sheets and clothes and just remembering our trips, the memories, her..."

"You went with her to Europe?"

"I did. The first and only time a poor piece of street trash like me will probably ever go. She paid for everything. And I mean everything. In the cities, we stayed in the best hotels. Rooms just opened up for her, carpets rolled out, faces smiling behind languages I didn't have a hope of speaking. It was only her second time, but she knew it like she'd grown up there. We spent every day together — all the way up until the night she disappeared." Then Nick's voice broke. "Is she dead? You have to tell me. Please tell me if she's dead. Please tell me anything."

"No man, she's not," Jared said.

The hopeful look that came over Nick's face made Jared turn away. It was easier for him to be honest about this one crucial point if they weren't making eye contact. "Well, her body is dead."

"What?"

"Come on, you had to have known she was."

"You just said she's not dead, then you say her body is dead? This whole thing stinks, and you need to tell me right now what the fuck is going on." Nick's voice was rising, bordering on a shout.

"You see all this, man?" Jared said. He raised his arms, gestured around the room. "You see all that out there, everything I have?" he paused for emphasis. "I've never had anything go wrong since that night. I quit my bullshit government desk job, never had to work another day. Never had to struggle. Never had to cope when something goes wrong. Because it doesn't go wrong. Everything slides exactly into place. The money, the relationships. Everything."

"What does this have to do with Flor?"

"You still don't get it, do you? Did you see Hakim's house? Did you see Jackie's house? Did you see Brocken's tour bus? It's everything we ever asked for. It all aligns, every single time. Every time we've wanted or needed anything, it happens for us. No effort. No expense. No wasted energy."

"Didn't happen for Daathioz," Nick said. He took a sip of whiskey, hoping it would ground him, hoping Jared would go on and explain everything.

"He broke the circle. It still worked for him, though."

"He was living in a tent, and he overdosed. He had nothing."

"He was always successful scoring. Never caught by cops. His dealers always answered, always were holding. He couldn't OD. He spent all his time doing exactly what he wanted to be doing. And trust me, it wasn't just drugs, although mostly it was."

The horror dawned on Nick. He remembered seeing Horace's corpse, how wrinkled and shriveled it was. The same way Jackie's corpse had. The same way Hakim and Brocken probably looked.

Jared watched Nick go white. "He looked just like Jackie, didn't he?" The door knocked again, opened. "God dammit, what?" Jared shouted.

"Oh, sorry, man, we're all here, we're gonna get started."

"I'll be out soon!"

"Oh, ok, man, sorry," Christian said, the door shutting softly.

Silence in the absence, and then Jared said into the quiet space of the office, "She's not dead, but she's not coming back."

"What the fuck does that mean? What did she get if you motherfuckers got all this?"

"We made a deal, swore oaths, signed a pact. We got everything we wanted. It was a fair trade, a fair fucking deal. I'm sorry that you somehow caught wind of this, got tangled in it. I'm sorry that she swindled you, too."

Nick swooned, clammy sweat under his collar. "I'm sorry, but I can't — I'm not following you."

"You went to Europe with her. What was she doing there?"

"I don't know, we went all over. She kept going to different churches, different markets. Having things blessed by priests. She just ran around all day. Sometimes she took me, sometimes she just left me to wander around museums and mausoleums."

"And what did you do at night?"

Nick blushed, remembering the nights, the touch of her body, the eagerness and enthusiasm of her love-making, and Jared caught it, barking out a cynical laugh. "What do you remember about her?"

"How worldly she was, how she'd seen and done everything. How hot she was," Nick blushed again at this last admittance.

"She was fucking hot, yes. But she was so jaded. Like she'd done everything in the world that there was to do."

"I remember feeling that way, too," Nick said, his voice dropping. "I felt inadequate. I wasn't sure why I was being blessed by this beautiful being's presence, why she wanted to share her life and love with me, and when it was taken, I wasn't sure how to return to a world without her."

"She got everything she wanted, too."

Nick turned to anger. "I want to know what happened!"

The guilt Jared thought he'd outrun was suddenly right behind him. "She was one of the best magicians I've ever worked with, and her results bear that out. You know where she got her money?"

"She has family back in Spain or something. Old money."

"Her family was piss poor. She got it from—" Jared said, starting and then freezing. Something came over his face, a grimace, and just as suddenly he was released, gasping. He stood, pulled at his pants, and headed for the office door.

"You alright?"

"Yeah, I'm fine, man."

Nick saw him decide against whatever he was about to say and felt the disappointment sweep across him as he realized this talk was at a sudden and inconclusive end. Then, Jared was out into the hallway. Nick headed out after him, the angst of unanswered questions burning his chest and neck.

Christian was sitting on a barstool getting a blowjob, and Nick stopped, distracted and disoriented.

"Hey, Jared, is this guy here for the party?" Christian said, sipping some wine and leaning back.

"No, I'm not." Something about the way the woman's mouth was wrapped around an erect penis like that, something squishy, something bodily, reminded him of those nights in Europe, wondering if this girl would spit into a goblet the way Flor had when he'd finished. A wave of despair and anxiety rushed through Nick. He peeled his eyes away and let his anger move him.

"How did Flor get her money?" Nick said, standing in close proximity to Jared and talking low.

"Magick," Jared said. The stirring dagger he used clanked against a fresh glass.

"None of this makes any fucking sense," Nick said.

"Tell me the truth. How did you find us?"

"She left a diary. Or like a journal or something. Most of it doesn't make sense, but there were loose papers. I found a list of names and numbers on it."

"Those had to be old. If she left names and addresses, they'd be ones we lived in before she died."

"I can show you the notebook."

"There's an AccurateStay in the next town over. Go and get a room. I'll meet you there tomorrow at noon, and we can talk more. And you'll show me the notebook."

"No point in talking if you're not going to fucking say any-thing."

Moaning sounds had started increasing throughout the big rooms. Jared palmed a pill into his mouth, chased it with a gulp of mint julep. Nick waited, but Jared said nothing, allowed nothing to come to his face.

"How can you even think about this bullshit party after seeing what you saw? What we both saw?"

"That's the second time I've seen it. I'll drown myself in the wine-dark seas of Dionysus that I might live again."

Nick stopped, his mind parted by what Jared had just said. The second time. Before he could amalgamate a picture of Flor sucked dry, body parts falling off in puffs of dust, he crossed the kitchen and grabbed his briefcase from the chair by the door. Nick opened it, remembering the book swap with a sudden surge of nervous fear. Knowing Jared was fading from this reality into the future in front of him, and to assuage his guilt at the theft, he asked an-other question as quickly as he could get it out.

"Mike Whittaker?"

Nick had Jared's attention again, and he waited, expectant. "See you tomorrow, man. Drive safe down that mountain road."

Jared held his glass up in cheers and headed to the couch. He stopped at the bar next to a fully engorged Christian and unabashedly stripped off his clothes. Nick tried to avert his eyes out of some instinct to be polite, but they lingered. On a thin, braided rope around Jared's hairy chest hung a simple golden ring.

Nick stepped out the door as Jared reached the couch in the middle of the room, a chorus of giggles silenced by a door closing.

The air was still, cold, and dark, the moon high in the sky above.

Nick drove as carefully as he could. He turned the radio on to try and distract himself as he passed the site of the accident, but no stations came through. He cranked the volume up anyway, the static loud and grating, while he stared at the lines in the road, not allowing himself to glance anywhere else.

Then he found himself in the hotel, lying on the bed, his whole body sore, exhausted. Sleep was a long time coming, Jacqueline's withered face visiting him over and over, sirens screaming past his room, accusing him from the window above the briefcase he was too tired to open. The remainder of his night was paved with the deep tar asphalt of nightmares.

SEVENTEEN

The moaning was muffled through the walls as Jared looked into the bright-lit vanity, one hand down his pants, gently grabbing himself and squeezing. The tenderness had not abated, and the sharp pain was getting worse. The general rules didn't allow clocks or watches at the orgy, preferring the experience to be "timeless," so he had no idea how many hours it had been hurting or how much the two orgasms and constant penetration made a difference. Probably made it worse.

Branches of apple trees knocked on the clouded bathroom window, tapping gently with the breeze. Jared remembered how little the trees had looked in his yard when he had planted them in a fit of theurgical benevolence. A three-day bender of weed, molly, mushrooms, wine, women, and song, while stopping every seventy minutes to perform a fervent invocation to Dionysus. They had started with seven-minute intervals but decided to space it out for hedonism's sake. At the end of it, he claimed an excruciating connection to Everything "with a capital E man, have you ever done Gematria on just the letter E?" and drove into the nearest town, bought four apple trees. The bewildered clerk helped this strange man with the wide eyes load the trees up, and Jared planted them with energy that belied three days of no sleep. He had failed to water them as ecstatically, but one had survived.

He turned the light off in the bathroom and rejoined the goings on. The red couch and surrounding areas of the living room was sprawled with bodies in varying states of rest or action. Jared grabbed a black satin robe lined with scarlet from a coat-rack and sat his draped body on one of the chairs at the foot of the library, smoking a blunt and watching. Christian was heading out of the pit, skin gleaming, penis semi-erect, and moved to sit on the chair next to Jared.

"Hey dude, you're welcome to sit, just ask that you put a robe on. The chair cushions, you know," Jared said.

"Oh, totally, man," Christian said, looking around. "Are there any?"

Jared passed the blunt to Christian, pointed at a coat rack. "Right there. You can use the same one for the rest of the party, I'll wash everything."

"You're a very courteous host. We really appreciate you hosting it here this time," Christian said, draping himself in a flash of emerald green. Jared thought suddenly of the book, the strange events of tonight.

"Yeah, dude, of course," Jared said from far away in his own thoughts.

"Hey, who was that dude? You both looked kind of bothered when you came in."

"I'm still not sure. I think he was like a friend of a friend."

"This your magick stuff?" Christian said, pointing at the bookshelves.

"Yeah, most of those books. I got other stuff up there, physics and math and some fiction."

"Why's that one sticking out?" Christian said, pulling a book from the shelf. Jared's crotch stung, and he played it up, trying to draw Christian's attention away, but Christian flipped through pages, ignoring Jared, who passed him the blunt hoping it would be a gesture that would entice Christian to put the book down.

"Hey, why's this blacked out?"

"What?" Jared said, trying not to sound surprised. A feeling cut through the roll of the molly and shivered down him like melting ice.

"Someone drew all over this figure in Sharpie. What are these? Like Pokemon?"

"I try to get you guys to do magick with me all the time, and now in the middle of this ,you're suddenly interested?" Jared said, trying another tactic. His heart was racing. Nick had switched the copies, and now he was going to look and see, and the silence that they had promised would be broken.

Luna walked up behind Christian, embracing him. The way her perky breasts rubbed against Christian's naked chest made Jared's penis twinge, and a stinging pain, electric and hot, shot up his spine. Christian closed the book, reshelved it, and kissed her sloppily. Jared rose from his chair. He had to call Nick right now, before another MDMA wave caressed him and sent the urgency down a serotonin river.

"Hey, don't get anything on my books, please," Jared said. He shuffled into his office off the small hallway, closed the door, and collapsed into the chair. His breathing was heavy, the pain intense. Nick would be staying where Jared told him to; it was the only motel remotely close. He opened a desk drawer and fumbled around. No phonebook. He slammed the drawer shut and cursed.

A black wave of bad feeling eclipsed the spirit of the party. Jared knew what would happen if Nick opened that book, saw that page, and uttered anything, even just read a word or a sentence out loud.

Jared groaned, tight and sore. Nausea pulsed low in his belly. The girl who'd been giving him a blowjob knew what she was doing, and he thought the tugging at his groin could be some leftover of that sensation. That's what the pain felt like it was doing; sucking him.

He leaned back in his office chair as his perineum jerked downwards in a rush of uncomfortable heat. The feeling of suction intensified, and the hurt flared, this time holding and not letting go. He disrobed, let the satin fall to the floor as he looked at himself, and saw a bulge of flesh on his groin. A cold sweat blossomed on his head and face as the pain magnified.

He felt his sweaty back sticking to the leather of the seat and then groaned with another painful yank. Jared tried to scream when he realized what was happening, what had happened to Jackie, Danta's phone call, the news of Brock, but something jerked from beneath him and took his breath downwards and out.

His hands clawed and gripped onto the armrests like he was clinging to a ledge. The suction of pain pulled him down, hard, and his grip slipped. The large sphere of flesh extruding from beneath his scrotum coned, growing outwards and bumping against

the wood of the desk, scratching against the sharp edge of a drawer.

When something put a dark container around him and the light of his office eclipsed, he thought he was passing out, but through the closing aperture of his vision ,he saw his body in the office chair growing smaller and farther away. He watched the flesh rend and melt, wrinkle and shrivel hideously. Then the darkness became total, and he knew where he was when he heard their voices, howling and dolorous.

EIGHTEEN

A knock on the hotel room door woke Nick from dreamless sleep. The sheets were tangled around his ankles, and the cup of water he'd put on the nightstand rested sideways against the far corner of the room, the spectral liquid in streams on the wall, glistening in the weak lamplight. The clock told him he'd been asleep for an hour.

Another knock, more insistent this time.

Nick extricated himself from the sheets and crossed the room. The hotel was too cheap to install a peephole, so he threw open the door. In front of him were the two men he'd seen in the SUV, silent and huge, eyes hidden behind mirrored sunglasses. They wore short-cut blonde hair and generic black suits. He waited for them to pull badges, to introduce and explain themselves. His chest hurt, and his vision swam before he realized he hadn't been breathing.

Instead of introductions, one of the men looked to his right and nodded. Nick heard thumping steps down the hallway, and a guy in a sharp suit, expensive haircut, and a smoothly-shaved aquiline face appeared behind the two men.

"Nichola Coultas?" the man said.

"Nick Kyle," Nick said, teeth clenching at the mention of his real name.

"Mike Whittaker," the man replied. The men in front of him parted, and Mike stuck his hand through the gap to shake Nick's. "Mind if I come in?"

Nick looked down unconsciously at his skinny, pale legs and stretched-out, dirty boxer shorts. Mike's eyes followed. "Oh, I'm sorry, I keep odd hours. There's a diner outside the motel in the parking lot. Please get dressed. My associates will wait and escort you. I'll see you in fifteen minutes," then he was gone.

Nick closed the door and crossed the room in a daze, the last twelve hours weighing on him. Jackie's corpse. All the information from Jared and Hakim. The story couldn't possibly be true. It was all bullshit. These dudes killed her and were covering it up with this wild occult story. Now Mike Whittaker had found him somehow, was at his hotel room door, the last person in Flor's journal alive, except for Jared. And then he remembered the sirens screaming past his room.

Nick got ready quickly, thinking over his cop shows, strategizing. Dressed, he opened the door again, clutching the briefcase to his side.

Outside his room, the two men stood sentry, silent and straight. Without a word they turned down the hall, and Nick followed them out of the motel. A two-minute walk through the damp night, and he sat down in front of Mike Whittaker, who had already ordered hot coffee.

Nineteen

Nick had hardly sat down when the food arrived. Mike got right to it and gestured with a gold Rolexed hand for Nick to eat, too, but Nick wasn't hungry. He poured and sipped coffee while watching Mike gorge himself.

Mike wiped his greasy face with a napkin, the sleeves of his silk camel suit flowing loosely around thick wrists. "Jared's dead," he said, his voice flat.

Nick blanched. His mind tried to slot what it had just heard and couldn't. Nick looked at Mike, sprawled in the center of a booth with two men framing him, sunglasses still on, and wondered what else they had done in his employ.

"Oh, these guys?" Mike asked. "Wasn't them. Hey, waitress," Mike waved at a woman behind the counter. He held up the coffee carafe and pointed at it. Nick drained his cup and set it on the edge of the table as the waitress poured refills and put the carafe down between empty plates. She turned to the two men in sunglasses.

"You gentlemen want anything?" They said nothing.

"They don't need much, I got them covered, thank you though," Mike said to the waitress, smiling. She didn't smile back, just turned and walked away.

"Hey," Mike said quietly, "Want a little nip?" He held his hands barely above the table, a dingy flask reflecting the harsh diner light. Nick hesitated. Mike unscrewed the lid, poured a measure of the liquid, the tarnished silver flashing as it overturned into his coffee, looking over Nick's shoulder like a naughty child, waiting for the waitress to catch him with this contraband.

She didn't turn around, and Nick accepted, against his better judgment. Mike poured a shot into Nick's coffee, tucked the flask back under the booth. Nick took a sip, let the hot, stinging liquid squirm its way down, crossing paths with his mood on its way up.

"Who are you?" Mike got out through his chewing, the noise filling the near-empty diner.

"Nick Kyle, private priv—"

"You're not a fucking private investigator, Nichola Coultas," Mike said through sausage. "You're not a fucking cop either. So, tell me, why do you keep ending up around all these bodies?"

"How do you know there are bodies?" The swiftness with which Nick volleyed this question, the perfect timing of it, thrilled him enough to energize his tired body.

"Why am I on your list?"

Nick couldn't resist the smirk. "What list?"

Mike slammed his hands down on the table, rattling all the dishes and spilling his coffee. Despite himself, Nick jumped. The sound was so loud in the diner; it made Nick look back at the waitress. Her eyes were on them, and her chest heaved as Nick watched her sigh deeply. He was relieved to hear her footsteps on the yellowing linoleum, hoping her presence would change the momentum.

"More coffee and a rag?" she said.

Mike nodded. "Sorry about the mess here, my guest just gave me some bad news. I'm a very emotive guy."

"Well, try not to emotive all over my floor, would you, hun?" She filled the coffee and left. Mike went back to eating, and the bad atmosphere resettled over the table.

Nick deflated. "How do you know Jared is dead?" Nick asked, sipping the coffee that he tried to steady by holding it in both hands.

"You didn't hear the sirens screaming past this place, headed up that hill?" Mike took another bite of over-easy egg. "You sure you don't want anything?"

Nick declined.

"If he ended up anything like Jackie—"

Nick sat up straighter. "How do you know about Jackie?"

"I know all of them, pal. My associates here followed her down the hill and watched her car crash."

Nick felt his face flush hot. "And why didn't they do anything when they 'watched her crash?'"

"Who do you think called the cops?" Mike said, chewing and staring Nick dead in the eye. Yellow yolk dribbled down the side of his mouth, which he quickly and neatly wiped away. "Do you at least have the book?"

Nick's heart was beating faster. He told himself to back off the coffee and breathe, and then asked, "What book?" He watched Mike's square jawline clench and his neck muscles tighten. Nick pulled at his own shirt collar and tried very hard not to look at the case beside him. "I'm not a big reader."

Mike laughed, shrugged, picked up his coffee and brought it to his lips, abruptly setting it back down when he changed his mind and decided to talk instead of drink. "My friends and I read it for a little book club we had going. I'm not sure they'd recommend it, though. It's a pretty demanding read."

Nick was very, very warm, and his heart was beating even faster than before. He felt an itch on his arm, scratched it. Mike was watching him intently, and when his eyes moved, Nick followed Mike's gaze down to a bright orange blotch spreading across his forearm. Nick scratched it again, and the room suddenly exhaled. The plates on the table tripled and shone with halos of rainbow diamonds, and then Nick was very far away, Mike calling for the check.

TWENTY

The place he stood was cavernous and dim. Candles burned in beautifully-wrought fixtures, but they only illuminated a small, thin strip — the darkness beyond the cowering flames was fertile. Nick plucked one from its holder's long, twisting arms, the wax dripping down his hand without the quick searing pain he'd expected. He held the weak light out in front of him and saw only a red, braided cord, its ends hidden as they stretched into the black.

Nick strained his eyes to see, fear rooting him to the spot. The red line shook and pulled taut as something moved towards him out of the darkness. On all fours, Flor crawled into the amber glow, naked but for the red string tied in a crisp bow around her neck.

Nick's sudden, fervent hope was for invisibility. He held the candle still with the idiotic thought that, if he pretended to be a candleholder, he would go unnoticed. The rope pulled her steadily forward in degrading parade. Her breasts hung limply, and Nick thought of teats drunk dry. Her hair was made up, tied back in neat braids, and her skin was clean and smooth, shining with oil. When they made eye contact, she smiled, sensuous and alluring. Something pulled her leash, then again more insistently, and she obeyed, continuing forward into the pool of black.

The strange sexuality of her self-assured and total submission conjured vague shapes of twisted eroticism out of the reach of his imagination. The sudden grasp of his mind's inability to go further called forth something that he could only comprehend as inadequacy, and he was jealous; jealous, sad, lusting, and terrified. Nick opened his mouth to call for her, to rescue her from unthinkable humiliations, but fear of the dark stopped him. Then, from out of the black came the low grunts he recognized from their lost nights. They rose to moans, then to long protracted affirmations of titillation and calls for continuance. The sounds of fucking heightened, headed towards climax, surrounding him and filling the huge space. Nick waited motionless in abhorrance for the penultimate lock of her voice that signaled the rictus of orgasm.

Through tears of maddened desire, he heard instead, "The strength of your Will at the moment of perfection shall determine the outcome, and the Word will be Made Flesh and Skin and Bone and Blood. All in pure Love. So mote it be."

"So mote it be," a group of voices answered.

"Begin."

A circle of the room lit in unison with a gong being rung. A cymbal hung from silvered rope in a frame of entwined serpents with gold-leaf scales and ruby eyes, vibrating through the stone and wood space with a deep sibilance. Surrounding Nick were pews, filled end-to-end with figures: parishioners. The harder he tried to focus on a single one of them, the fuzzier and more opaque the figure became. They stared forward dumbly, concentrating on something in front of them: Flor, atop a stone altar.

Nick just barely glimpsed the swollen hoods of the flower between her legs before robed figures moved inside the circle and blocked his view.

Nick's desire and envy drove him forward. He stopped on the edge of the shadows and tried to avoid being seen by the robed figures or plucked by the monstrous lurkers in the blackness. Nick felt no comfort or certainty in his position and blew his candle out in a child's attempt at hiding.

Movement at the altar called Nick's attention. One of the robed figures was now standing behind Flor. It removed its hood, exposing Jared's blank face, his lips moving despite his distant stare.

Flor was silently writhing, hips thrusting and grinding in the air, when Jared's voice abruptly rose with placatory invocations. The tone grew into a crescendo and crashed into silence. Nothing happened.

Jared paused, turned a page of the book in front of him, and began a second, harsher command. Another robed hand, black, flung something onto burning charcoal. The material landed on the hot coals and flared, popping, the smoke rising rapidly and fleeing. Some of it bounced atop the altar, and Flor jerked her legs away from it as if burned.

As one of the robed figures in the circle raised their hands. Jared's voice was loud, and he held a knife in his hand that caught the light. Nick could see Flor clawing at her neck, trying to get her fingers underneath the red ribbon tightening around her neck like a ligature, her face wracked in prolonged, frightened orgasm.

Then, with dolorous annunciation, the air darkened outside the circle, curdling. The scattered candelabras lost all their light, surrendering to the rapidly chilling air.

It wasn't a voice he heard — it was more intrusive than vocalizing.

Nick's inner monologue, that familiar and comforting sound he knew to be him, had been replaced. Against the recently pitched black of the room, a faded, green smear like a badly developed Polaroid arrived directly above the altar. Nick was unable to focus on the apparition: he turned his head to look at it straight on, but the closer his vision came to the center of it, the more it camouflaged itself with unlight.

The razor-tipped pit of ululations grew and took up more frequency, the air thinning under their greedy consumption. The saliva in Nick's throat turned to acid and, when he swallowed an involuntary gulp, it warmed his intestinal tract with sour nausea. The figures amongst the pews rose to standing on spectral feet.

"Terms first," Flor said. She was calm now, sitting upright and beautiful on the altar. Nick's anxiety whipped him, and he whimpered aloud, instantly regretting announcing his terrified presence. The blur of the darkness around the figures in the circle sharpened, the robes straightening in posture with an electric spasm.

Then, as he remembered her doing in the heat of their passion, she simply lay down and spread her legs, raising her arms towards the miasma, assuming the god form of Erotic Love. In a flash, Nick saw an amalgam of the sex they had shared and felt hot shoots of covetousness as the dark cloud lowered on her welcome.

Right before it covered her, Jared plunged the dagger into her heart.

Flor began to tremble, the shock unable to be sung from lungs quickly filling with blood. The dark outside the circle shifted peripherally, and the glow above the altar deepened colors, coming fuller into vision. The candles jumped and began burning fiercely. In front of him, the congregants began swaying in dissensus — one of them leaned too far, and its robe caught in a candle. As it swayed, it knocked heads with another figure, and the fire jumped, consuming the crazed figures in the pews, one by one, as they tilted and wobbled into each other.

As the faithful became torches and brightened the room, it was easier to see the barely transparent claws of three hands reaching down from the insane, unintelligible shadows and gently grabbing the ribbon. Flor's naked body was lifted into the air, but she was smiling, laughing giddily as she ascended. The blazing heat of the spreading fire warmed the cold, wet tears on Nick's weeping face.

All at once, a gold light above the altar shone and projected a vision: a castle, resplendent in white, glowing like Heaven. Out of the turrets spilled piles and piles of gold coins and shining jewels. The huge doors of the castle opened, and on large wooden tables sat huge feasts, crystal bowls full of powders, golden goblets overflowing with red liquids, and green vegetable matter in solid nuggets, bodies twisted in strange displays and parodies of lovemaking. Against the interior walls, more people were chained, subjected to inhuman tortures, while looks of rapture and terror swept across their bloodied faces. Treasure and pleasure morphed and transposed, squirming around and through each other, hopeless of solidity, a maniac kaleidoscope of earthly gratification and hellish ruin.

The circled members' hoods had slipped from their heads, and Nick recognized them all. Horace was the first to break from the circle. As he fled, the castle formed eyes, slanted with hatred. The drawbridge became rows of sharpened teeth, gnashing in gluttonous rage at the insolence of attempted flight. They bit down on the fleeing figure who reached out to Nick for pitiful, unconsummated mercy.

The others were now scrambling for escape, visages of abject loss and fright cramping their features as they attempted flight. The clawed fingers descended again from the black air, reaching, grabbing, catching, and hauling them back up. Flor simply floated in through the doors of the castle and disappeared. Something in the air screamed Nick's name as a feeling of sharp grabbed him around the shoulders and ribs, grasping him easily and pulling him the air perfumed with the sulfur reek of snuffed candles.

Nick heard the voice again, all around and through him, calling his name, modulating from higher shrieks to lower guttural growls. Then, the voice became Flor's and curled on itself again, became man deep and then child high, and someone was shaking his shoulder.

"Nick. Nick," the voice said. Mike stood above him, holding a briefcase under his arm. Nick was struggling to breathe, exhaling, spitting, and yelling. When hands dragged him upright, he lifted his leg, trying to hide the painful erection pressing and surely outlined against his pants. "Hey, hey man, stop yelling," Mike said as Nick shook himself awake and tried to bring his legs under him to stand and run. They buckled, but he felt two people at each of his arms, pulling him steadily up. He looked down at the brown, solid wood of the pew.

Mike stepped into an aisle and performed a parody of genuflection. He raised the familiar-looking briefcase up and made a motion of cheers at the crucified figure on the wall.

Nick recognized the case as his own. He was turned around forcibly, facing the two heavy wooden castle doors from his nightmare. Before he could protest, he was lifted and half-dragged down the aisle, then shoved, screaming, through them into the harsh, abrasive daylight, with powerful hands grabbing his head and preventing him from looking back.

TWENTY-ONE

The center of the leather seat was a mass of tiny perforations, and the aftershocks of whatever was slipped into his coffee made it ripple. Nick stared, watching them shift in and out of legible glyphs — they were trying to tell him something, but he hadn't paid enough attention to Flor's ramblings to know how to read them.

His eyes welled, but his body was miserably dehydrated; instead of crying, he just let out a pitiful yelp as the back of the seat shimmied again.

"That'll wear off in an hour or two, and you won't feel so depressed," Mike said from the front passenger seat. One of the suited men drove, his head staring straight out the windshield. The other one sat next to and facing Nick, with no seatbelt on, watching him, waiting.

Through a dry mouth, Nick tried some words, simple ones he could croak. "Why a church?"

The man next to him handed him a water bottle. Nick looked at it as a wave of self-loathing and distrust crashed into him.

Mike unbuckled his seat belt and started wrestling himself out of his tailored jacket. "We tried to have a Mass said over the book. One of the things you gotta do to work it. But the old man fuckin' refused.."

Nick felt like he should have cared about the book, should have started asking questions. "You need to drink some water," Mike said. Nick looked again at the proffered bottle held by an untrembling hand; something about the way the man's suit fitted against the skin of his wrist made Nick's stomach roll with nausea, like the fabric grew out of it, instead of sitting on top.

Nick turned his head to the window. They were headed out of a large town, traveling now through the industrial outskirts, a landscape portrait of perpetual construction sites and concrete towers belching smoke.

"You been out all day, it's four o'clock already. We put the dose too high, sorry about that. Precautions. You sure whined a lot. Shit seemed to bring you nightmares like a bat to fruit, you kept saying her name. What's your interest in Flor anyway? You fucking her?" Mike put his arms up to himself, wriggled them around on his back, and moaned. "Oh, Flor, Flor, mi amor!" Mike laughed.

"I think she was fucking me," Nick said, surprised by the shock of frankness. "I loved her, and I'm pathetic, and I could never attain to someone so perfect and knowing and confident. Nowhere close." This confession opened a gate, and the tears flowed out, heavy and warm.

"Hey, man, you need to chill out. Just got the moonflower blues." Mike reached into the glove box, retrieved a joint and a lighter. "Here, this will help cushion the fall a little bit." Mike passed Nick the joint, but Nick refused it. "Suit yourself, man," Mike said. The passenger window slid down, the cabin rumbling with the epiphany of the wind. The cloud of smoke rolled into the cabin and out the window. Beneath the skunk fragrance, Nick could smell sulphur and burning asphalt.

"Where are we going?" The man was still holding the bottle out to Nick with no sign of fatigue, so Nick took it and unscrewed the cap. By the way the bottle resisted opening, he figured it wasn't tampered with. His mouth felt so dry, he didn't care if it was. The cool liquid didn't go down easily, catching against his roughed throat. Nick coughed and spluttered.

"I don't know what it's called man. 'The Place' is what Jared called it."

"You were there that night."

"On a total whim."

"What the hell does that mean?"

"I used to buy weed from Jared, and some other stuff, sometimes. I just happened to be at his place one night to pick up, and he mentioned it to me. They needed an extra. I asked him when, he said they were about to leave. I hopped in the car." Nick noticed Mike's voice lowering as he went on, and he craned to hear him over the rush of air.

"Had you ever done any of what they were doing?" Nick asked. The anxiety had spiked again, and his total lack of ability to speak this language had dunked him back into a pool of inadequacy.

"No. My only exposure was Jared, but he talked about it all the fuckin' time. Every time we hung out, it was like two hours of crazy bullshit from that Order they'd all been in. I look back and marvel at how I happened to be buying from Jared that night. Almost like it wanted me to be there."

"But you were out there with—"

"Yeah," Mike said. Then he went quiet for a long minute to stare out the window. The highway was wide open in front of them, the flat plains emerging.

"Where were you? Where did this happen? What—?"

"I'll show you."

TWENTY-TWO

Mike had pulled out a copy of the book and was idly flipping through the pages, looking from figure to figure, and then stopped. "I think it was this one," he said.

Nick leaned forward to see. The driver glanced in the rear-view mirror, and the man next to him leaned forward simultaneously, following Nick. The eerie way they moved sent another ripple through him, and he didn't look, didn't feel worthy, didn't feel like he was ready to see.

"Yeah, this is it," Mike said. The joint smoldered in the ash-tray; when Mike moved, it disturbed the still air, the thin smoke swaying around, coalescing into more signs lost on Nick. From the compartment in the door, Mike pulled another copy of the same book, flipped it open, and stopped on a page with a large, black splotch in the middle.

"Yeah, ok," Mike said and closed the books.

"Will you tell me what the fuck—"

"The day after — I had kind of an epiphany." Mike laughed. "It was like a program turned on and started running me. I was frenzied. I started all these shops and businesses, wading through opportunities, picking and choosing, buying and selling. It was like I couldn't fail. And one day, I just woke up and had sold everything. For a lot of money. Everything I did went off without a hitch. The syncs, the luck, the right places I happened to be in, the right times."

Nick chuckled bitterly, remembering the way Hakim and Jared had described their runs the same way. Where had Flor's luck been?

"I had a dream about Flor the night I sold them," Mike said just as Nick thought her name. "I got blind drunk, lines and lines and lines, and usually I don't sleep that well with all that shit up my nose, but when she showed up, everything was crystal clear. I'd never done this before, I didn't know how it worked. But that night, with her, in that dream, I got a glimpse."

Nick could see Mike shiver and adjust in his seat, rolling his shoulders back. The sound of his joints popping audibly in the quiet car covered the frisson, but only briefly before it settled back, bleak and quiet. "The next day, I made it my business to get rid of the book. Found out there were plans to publish it."

"So Daathioz bought all these and kept one for himself?"

"No. I bought the publishing company. Paid them a lot. Then I put Jackie on the board, made it look like she'd gotten there herself. Turns out the books were printed and in the warehouse, just sitting there. Something was wrong with the spelling on the spine or some shit, and the publisher wasn't happy with the quality, so they were waiting for the printer to repress before they went for binding. None of them made it out. We destroyed every single one of them, cancelled and refunded all the preorders, and answered no questions from anyone. I paid Daathioz to break into the printer's office and destroy all the equipment and plates. Wasn't hard to make it look like a junkie, considering he fucking was one. The only ones left were the advance copies she'd sent to her friends. I was fucking furious when I found that out."

Mike tapped the driver on the shoulder. "Another five miles and turn left." He then continued to Nick, "I've been tracking those down. Hakim and Jackie destroyed theirs, Jared had Daathioz's." Mike held both copies up, "Nice move, by the way. And you had Jared's, the original copy that he grabbed before he ran from the fire."

"Fire? What fire?"

"What do you actually know about what happened?" Mike asked, quieter.

"I know none of you are supposed to be talking about this is any way."

Mike was silent for a minute. "That's all it asked for." Mike touched his head, "it was like a drill in my brain."

"What was it? Everyone keeps saying it? What is it?"

Mike pointed at the book. "That's what it doesn't want you to know. That's why Daathioz blacked his out. In my dreams, it's always different, and she's always right in the middle of it. A harem girl wrapped in the coils of a cobra, or a cow with snakes for horns and tits. One night, she was a little girl on a bike going down a hill, out of control, and every time I got close to the bike, tried to catch her, she would laugh and go faster."

"Flor."

"She was so hot. That body. Wars have been fought for women with less than she had. But you could tell just by looking at her she'd done everything fun there was to do in the world. You'd never impress a chick like that. I think that's why she chose to do what she did," Mike said. He pointed ahead to a road that branched off from the highway and said something to the driver.

"What do you mean 'she chose?'"

"Yeah, that road. Turn left." The car slowed down to make the turn, and Mike looked out the window. "Yeah, this is it, I think."

Nick asked the question again more forcefully.

"You're not a private investigator. One of those would have put some pieces together by now."

"Flor is dead."

"And everyone around her is rich and perfectly set in life. Was rich and perfectly set in life. You saw the houses, you saw the lifestyles."

"What does that have to do with 'what she chose?'"

"Oh, fuck's sake, man. How much did you know about her?"

"Never as much as I wanted."

"We're getting close, so it's your choice: you can write poetry or ask questions."

Nick looked around. The landscape was arid and desolate, nothing in sight but blank earth. "What happened that night? Tell me the whole thing."

"They summoned a demon or some kind of spirit, and we asked for our wildest desires."

"And Flor's desire was to be murdered?"

"Try again."

As it dawned on him, he nauseated, the insight blooming into words, remembering the dreams. "She asked—"

"For her wildest desire."

"To — go with it?"

Mike laughed and rolled down the window. The haze of marijuana smoke, tranquil and motionless, was sucked forcibly out into the air, dissipating behind them. Mike pointed and then said, "It looked just like that. Watch the smoke." He laughed again, blew more smoke out the window. Nick didn't like the sound of that second laugh.

"I don't—"

"None of us knew. Well, Jared knew, he was the one with the knife. But you could see it in her eyes, man. She was jaded when she first showed up and ecstatic when she lay down on the table."

"No, Jared didn't say he—"

"He plunged it right into her heart. Like they'd practiced. Nailed it on the first shot. You know PTSD? The shit soldiers get, or people traumatized? I think that's what happened to me, instantly. I don't remember feeling scared or angry. Like it was just a play, like in a theater. There was a clarity — I could see some kind of tail or something in the smoke of the incense. My eyes were so sharp I could see its origin point on the charcoal. I remember looking around, and everyone had the same kind of look on their face. Wide eyes. I remember waiting for the blood to spurt, like a vampire movie. It didn't, though. It kind of bubbled up. Like a well. Most of the time, I can't even shut my eyes at night without that looping itself in my head." Mike pointed ahead and tapped the driver. "See those trees? Head for those."

Nick looked ahead and saw the copse. It looked like someone had planted a ring of trees in the middle of nowhere as a joke. Just one stand of giant trees against miles and miles of absolutely nothing. He had tears in his eyes that reluctantly ran down his cheeks when he blinked.

"You — you killed her for money?"

Mike put his head in his hands and sighed. "No, you're not listening. We didn't kill her. Jared stabbed her in the heart, true. I know that sounds like murder. But she offered herself."

"Like, assisted suicide?"

"Jesus fucking — man, no. She was like a gift. Like the shaved and lotioned women who offer themselves to rock stars. Their bodies in exchange for a night in the presence of something truly bigger than them. And maybe the guy likes 'em, takes 'em on tour. Takes them to his multiple houses, drives them around to fancy dinners and coke parties in red shiny cars. Maybe. If they're a good enough offering. You get what I'm saying? She wanted it."

At the monstrous impact of Mike's construction of events, Nick collapsed under his grief. He wept as the dream that hadn't been a dream flooded back. He felt regret and love, stupidity and admonishment, passion and disgrace. He remembered how absolutely smitten he had been with her and how dull and simple he'd felt in her presence more than once. One night in a motel by the Vatican, after they'd had sex, the composition of their joining filled him with golden tender light, and he'd told her he loved her. He felt it immensely, knew it to be patent reality, with his whole being. He could hear, even now, the pity in her voice as she'd laughed and left for the bathroom.

He cried, pitifully, like a child who had a toy stolen by a bully. Then, she'd realized he was serious. Her attitude had changed, softened, but not enough that she'd say it back. He'd known then how little her regard was for him, which, over the trip, had been eclipsed by her will and desire to run her enigmatic errands during the day.

With the information from Mike and the past few days, he now stood in the bitter, ugly light of the truth of her undertakings. The shiny brass candlesticks from the vision, and all the decorations of that wretched room; she'd been having them made, and she was using him for sex in order to mingle their fluids for consecrating these stupid little trinkets. He'd felt humiliated then, and the flush of it reddened him even now, sitting in this stinking car and sinking into his seat, crushed by the debasement.

She'd opened the world to him, a world that he would never see or experience again. For not the first time, he wondered why she'd picked him. And then he did the one thing he knew she would have despised the most. The one thing she would have loathed him for. He pitied himself.

"I know what you're thinking, but I think 'whore' is the wrong word here," Mike said. "She wasn't a whore. Well, maybe she was, maybe that's where she got all her money. But she offered herself. Small consolation now, but the difference is a big one."

Nick sobbed, letting the answers he had been handed slip through his fingers and fall to the floor mats, wet and heavy with shameful tears.

When the car turned and stopped, the driver jumped out and moved to Nick's door. He opened it at the same moment the guy next to him grabbed Nick's arm and pushed him into iron-fisted custody.

Mike was already headed towards the building: a small edifice of stone and wood that reminded Nick of a Renaissance Festival, some poor modern approximation of the castles and fortresses of Europe. He felt the poisoning of nostalgia, the dissolving anamnesis of those private tours, the bereavement of hope.

The closer they got, the more the building loomed, growing into something menacing and prison-like.

"Right this way, gentlemen," Mike said. Nick watched as Mike produced three keys, swiftly opening three locks at differing heights of the door, and then he stepped through and was swallowed into darkness by the maw of the portal. The two men dragged Nick to the door, and he gulped as it swallowed them, too.

The inside was charred black, thick with total murk. "What are we doing here?" Nick asked. In response, a piece of cloth was placed over Nick's mouth, and he felt a sudden, sharp blow to his neck.

When he woke up, the candles were blazing.

TWENTY-THREE

Standing here now, staring into the dark, Mike could remember it like it was yesterday. His mind evoked it easily and projected the flashbacks on the charred black walls. Candlesticks, candleholders, incense thuribles of shining bronze suspended from chains on holders of equally bright brass. The way the light from the candles shone off the surfaces of the ornate setup and gave the room an eerie sheen, while Mike tried to piece together how the hell he had gotten there.

The conversation he had with Jared at his place, this magic stuff — no matter how you spelled it, which Jared was more than happy to drone on about — had never been Mike's bag, but Jared said they needed an extra for something they were doing. Mike was bored, and he didn't have work the next day, so he shrugged and agreed.

The piece that clicked it together for Mike was the promises Jared had made about the potential outcome. Not necessarily money, Jared said. "Wealth." Jared had explained that money was wealth, but wealth wasn't necessarily money, nuances that had been lost on Mike. He didn't even know what he would do with wealth, but he knew more money meant not working, so he'd agreed with Jared and went along.

"Leave him in a corner and go get the equipment."

Nick's body was dropped unceremoniously, and the footsteps echoed out of the building, back into the fading afternoon. Mike's heart beat a tattoo as he approached the door and flung it open. He felt his head whirl as he stared into the black, then stepped in. It was spooky and quiet, and then the clattering behind him made him jump as his two subordinates hustled large black bins into the room.

When their frames shadowed the door, he could almost see Floriana suddenly standing there, her presence thundering.

He remembered how hot she was, skin perfect, clean, expensive clothes absolutely dripping in gold jewelry, and palo santo scent wafting off her as she joined the group. Mike stood rooted as the men shuffled in and out and watched it all unfold again.

"Is this the seventh?" she asked, without taking her eyes off Mike.

"Yeah, Doug backed out," Jared said.

"Is he fasted?" Flor asked coldly. Mike hadn't eaten since the night before, and Jared told him that counted.

"Uh, yeah," Mike said. His blind confidence had gotten him plenty of places before, but he was finding it difficult to use it now. Flor held his stare firmly by the reins, and he felt hypnotized. Mike couldn't have looked at Jared for backup even if he wanted to. Not with such a creature in front of him.

"The circle is drawn," Hakim said, entering the room. "Oh, hi, Flor."

"Is everything set?" Flor said.

"I think so," Hakim said. "Hey, this a great find, Flor. Thanks for scouting out the location."

"Took me a week of flying," Flor said.

"You can fly a plane?" Mike had asked, skeptical, trying to use sarcasm to fend off the lack of self-confidence that this beautiful woman had invoked in him. She didn't look back or answer the question, and Mike felt a sudden ache for her attention.

"Hey, Flor, that antechamber you asked for is cleaned out and ready," Jackie said eagerly.

"Good. I'll be in there preparing. We have twenty minutes until the moon stations. I want to be chanting in fifteen," Flor said. In a whirl of what Mike could only describe as a heavy mist, Flor retreated from the room.

"What's her deal?" Mike said after waiting a long time to make sure she was out of earshot. He was slightly dizzy, like he had just re-entered his body, and he felt Flor's absence physically.

"She's rich," Daathioz said, grabbing a robe from the box. "It does something to your brain." Mike had hated that skinny twit from the first moment he saw him. Hated the stupid nickname he'd given himself, hated the way his greasy hair was slicked back into a ponytail, hated his nasally voice and his taped glasses.

"So, she just gets to talk to people like that?" Mike said.

"She funded all of this, these candles are from the Pontiff's own collection," Jackie said, turning away from him and removing her black shirt.

"How'd she get candles from the Pope?" Mike asked, glancing at her back and then turning toward Jared. His modesty surprised him, but his body was yearning for someone else.

"She's rich," Brocken said, tossing a robe on an old, dusty chair in the corner. Mike remembered the way Brocken had looked standing in that black robe, more upright, almost proud, his clothes in a neat pile beside him. Then the black guy had tossed Mike a robe.

"Hurry and get dressed, man," Hakim said. Mike pulled the thing over his head, got slightly lost in it before he found the arms and neck, and then the cloth slid down effortlessly.

"Uh, uh. Clothes off," Daathioz said.

Mike didn't hesitate. He took off his clothes inside the robe, and when he lifted his leg to take off his socks, Brocken pointed. "All your clothes, man, underwear too."

Mike had just enough time to wonder what he really gotten himself into when the gong was struck.

Standing again in the empty and blackened chamber, Mike could see Flor, lying there, the dagger flopping around in her chest as her breath slowly quit.

The feelings overtook him, squeezing. When he finally punched back through the memories, he saw the two men standing at the entrance, one holding Nick's limp form.

The book gripped by his cramping fingers had held more than just a spirit list. There were spells in there to find treasure or your future lover, spells to curse your enemies with failed crops and famished sows, and there was a spell that summoned two assistants in forms most helpful to the petitioner.

He waved them in and began setting up.

TWENTY-FOUR

Through slowly clearing sight, Nick could see the bright flares of candles reflecting off highly polished candleholders. He blinked, looking up at the charred black ceiling, panicking as he tried to tell nightmare from reality.

Mike's voice came from behind his head. "Oh good. I was going to do it without you, but I'm glad you're up."

Nick tried to look behind him, felt something thin holding his neck firmly. He could only see Mike's head, which smiled an upside-down smile. "When you've gone through all the rigmarole once and contacted a spirit, it's a lot easier to get them back on the line. That's what I've heard, anyway."

By the way his arms failed to follow his movement, Nick knew he was tied down. A scuffling sound on the floor, and then Mike was standing beside him, clutching a dagger that glimmered in the yellow candlelight. Nick struggled, felt his bare skin tear against the ropes, useless. Adrenaline curdled his stomach.

"You're the last one who knows anything about this. Think about that. In the entire world, you're the only one. How many people did we drive past on our way out here? How many people know where you are right now, know what you went looking for?" Mike was moving around him, close enough for Nick to smell his breath. With a small sound like a whispered zip, Nick felt his three-day-old, sweat-stained shirt being lifted away from his skin.

"It wanted silence. That's it. And somehow you got so twisted around some pussy that you caused all this death."

"I didn't have anything to do with their deaths," Nick said, but Mike caught the lack of conviction in his voice.

"You're pretty pathetic. To think Flor made this all happen with someone like you. Do you think any of these people would be dead without you showing up and asking questions?"

"You said you didn't even know her."

"I didn't, but I know what happened that night. I know what my life became. I know what their lives became. Imagine trying to sit down at a beautiful steak dinner and not being able to concentrate on it because there's a rat running through your walls, asking stupid questions, and making a fucking racket. Wouldn't you want to rip that rat out of the wall and nail it to the front door so the rest of 'em get the message?"

Nick squirmed against the ropes again and then gave up. No one even knew where he was. They would never find this place, and there would be no one left to ask. No grieving family. He thought of his schizoaffective mother, locked away in that "assisted living facility," the father that he never knew, the one who had run away when Nick was just a few days old. He was alone, and he would die alone.

Mike was saying something Nick couldn't make out, his voice exhaling a phrase like he was trying to expel snake venom. The candles flickered, and the walls and ceiling went a darker dark. The dream swarmed his thoughts, blocking out everything. Nick whimpered, lashing his head around in small, useless maneuvers.

Mike moved again and roared a word Nick didn't understand. He knew from the direction of the horrible yell that Mike was moving now in a circle, stopping at different locations. When the loudness echoed, the candles shone like torches.

"Please, I—"

"There's nothing you can offer me, Nichola," Mike said, spitting out his name. "All I want is your silence. It would be a great gift to me, though I'm not sure you'll be a great gift to it," Mike said, rotating back around, standing behind Nick's head now. "Maybe you'll even get to make a fool of yourself in front of her again."

Mike whispered another word, and Nick felt cool spittle on his forehead. He was fully paralyzed and felt piss dripping down his leg, then Mike was at his side, exhaling a word with a soft breath, erotically.

The cracked black ceiling above him lost its form, swallowed by churning darkness that smoothed out the farther it spread from its whirling center. A wind blew cool through his sweat-matted hair, and on it, carried through the stygian gloom, was Flor's sweet voice, soft and gentle. And inviting.

Then the room exploded into cacophony. Voices in ugly, dead languages chattered stupidly, mixing with the outcries and raspings of disturbed animals in violent throes of killing and dismemberment; sounds like scratches, ripping, tearing, noises of curling fire, and the angry refusals to accept death rended through his ears, threatened to slough his skin.

He strained against the ropes, desperate to bring his hands up to cover his ears and stop the noise from tapping further into his brain. He gripped the stone beneath him and felt the blood drip off his fingernails as they scratched desperately and broke.

The noise came to a sudden halt, the silence suffocating. Nick felt the quiet press him like stones, stealing his breath. The strangulation ignited a different panic through his body, and he wished that the blare would return and relieve him.

The darkness above and around him enclosed further, snuffing out candles in palpable rage. Then the voice was in his head, a question forming in his mind that Nick couldn't answer — he had no idea what he was doing here.

But then he did know, the feeling overwhelming him.

It took a horrible moment for his brain to make sense of Mike, who was above Nick and raising the dagger. "That's why I offer you this! This man is the cause of your outrage, and with my gift to you, I offer you the silence you crave!"

Nick knew with a deep sense in his squirming reptilian brain that the waiting should be over, the time to act here and present. What are you waiting for? The feeling said. So Nick acted, muscles straining, body thrusting with a last burst of will. The ropes held him firmly, and he went nowhere, did nothing but sag, bound and powerless. His eyes couldn't even cry.

Then the dagger came down.

The burning was minor, and when he lifted his head, he watched something wiggle and vibrate with the tension of his taut muscles. The room around him had become bright, and with the light came sensory activation, Nick could feel the pressure now, a little sharper, his chest warming, liquid. When he opened his mouth to speak, the noise came out like the hiss of a flat tire.

Mike was shouting.

"There! I give him to you! You are now nested among the traitors who bothered you! I ask for the same! I want to be left alone with what I've been given by you, by what I have grown so grateful for!"

The candles guttered, dropping the light in the room. With another attempt at speech, Nick felt something warm and wet spray from his mouth. Instead of talking, what came out was a gurgle. When he felt himself choking, liquid pooling in his throat, his panic rose with a final tumescence.

"Take him! Take this ugly thing, who has betrayed your great rewards and patronship!" Through Nick's fading vision, he saw the light in the room change and knew instantly that Mike had said the wrong thing. Nick's eyes were slowly closing, the room narrowing around him, but he heard Mike begin to question, and then to beg, and then his screams became unambiguous.

Nick felt himself going backwards through the last few days and the cold spots on his body, lines of icy manipulation. He didn't have the energy to lift his head but could loll it and strain through his peripheral vision and see the ghostly, shriveled corpses around him, caressing him.

Backwards through his obsession with finding Flor, backwards through his obsession with Flor, backwards through meeting her, seeing her for the first time. Nick saw his life: memories and events, loves and fucks and fights and peak experiences that by their very weight had embedded themselves in his mind.

Something about Flor had brought his life to this apex experience, something he longed for. A mediocre existence, no great passions or persuasions. The things he had seen the past couple of days had rivaled anything he'd seen in the last four decades, and the only reason he'd seen it was Flor, because she'd brought him, had been with him, had taken him and shown him a life he so desperately wished to keep. And then she had disappeared and taken those hopes with her.

His thoughts swallowed their tail, and if he could have laughed at how pathetic and inconsequential his life had been, he would have.

The burning heft of the dagger had spread across his chest, heavier, extremely tactile now in Death's proximity.

Out of the corner of his vision, he saw a movement like flapping. With his last, sad spark, he hoped he would be heading to her, wherever she was. A Voice, gruff and scratching, assured him that he would be headed no such place.

Nick's breath shallowed as he tried to reach out, trying and failing to scream her name into the void.

His last conscious thought was the memory of her laughing when he told her he loved her. It scored him now like a honed, hot razor of utter rejection. He screamed into the closing, tunneled void, "I love you, Flor! Flor! Help me! I love you!"

He heard her laugh, the same laugh he heard in Florence, and then he died.

Mike watched from the floor, twisted in torture, envious as Nick's last breath expelled. He didn't know if Nick was headed the same place he was, and the voice thundered laughter through his head, orgasmic cruelty.

Mike's feet arched as he was hooked, pelvis lifting as he was pulled, head and neck dragging on the floor. He was crying, weeping as the force brought his legs crashing against the altar where they splintered and broke, then Mike was dragged into the air, suspended. He looked down, saw Nick's body: splayed, shrunken, and nearly fossilized.

Then Mike was dropped headfirst onto the altar, face disintegrating from the force. As he began to drown in his own blood, the blistering pain began in his back. The light around his vision had darkened, he felt something trying to pry him out, and his last thought was of clams.

The room narrowed and he heard the screaming voices of the people he remembered so well, the ones whose faces he'd seen in the brief snatches of sleep he'd been allowed.

His ribs broke, splintering, and his spine moved aside politely. As Mike left his body, he looked down. The room was exactly how it had been left, the book on its stand in front of the altar, the candles burning. He tried to close his eyes when he was shoved through the shadows, but something sharp and cruel held them open, and a vista of depravity consumed him.

TWENTY-FIVE

The door had been propped open, but the bright daylight refused to enter. Two identical men with long blond hair and matching jogging suits entered and headed straight to the two bodies. One was shriveled on the altar, turned almost inside out; the other lay broken on the floor, sand-colored, with all the hallmarks of mummification. The two men both bent down to the bodies.

"No, leave them," a voice said from the door, his mellifluous voice accented with Spanish.

A strong, square jawline with thick black hair framing his face stared into the room, taking in the scene. When he saw the book, he walked in and picked it up gingerly.

"Find the keys to the other car." The two men bent over the bodies. The corpse on the altar lifted easily, and one of the blonde men rummaged through its pockets. Finding the keys, he held them aloft, jingling them to get the man's attention.

"Very good. Both of you take the car and find a forest. Drive the car deep into it and get lost. Then your work is finished." They dropped the corpse without ceremony in a puff of dust.

The man waited until he was alone before looking around.

The charred building made for quite the uncanny space, he admitted. It must have looked absolutely stunning when the full ritual was set and working. He felt the book under his arm, heavy and warm, soft leather boards wrapped around hard miracles. By the looks of the corpses, they'd gotten it to work.

That little bitch kept the book in pretty good condition, he thought. When he re-shelved it in his family's ancestral library, it wouldn't even look out of place. He smiled at the thought.

He'd spent the last few years trying to track Floriana down, grudgingly admiring the way she'd managed to leave little trace.

His attempts at contacting her had turned up nothing. Her family said she'd been murdered, location unknown. His own grandmother's ire had been great, threatening him with more than just being cut from the will.

But he'd found her. Found her mother and her father, who had sobbed. They'd begged him to help, pleaded for him to find any answer for what had happened. He'd promised them with sugary lies that he'd find the answers. But he already knew they would never really hear the answer, never be able to admit such truths into their tiny hovel of accepted reality.

Better to let them cry.

He snapped the pages shut with a satisfying smack, and he felt his palm grow warm with its proximity. Maybe this would put him back in the good graces of his grandmother, that sullen matriarch. Maybe.

He left the tomb quietly without looking back.

ABOUT THE AUTHOR

Thomas Sachs is a writer and lives at the edge of the forest with a dark-haired woman in a tower of spider-haunted mystery. He loves books, films, music, practicing magic, and lifting heavy weights.

ABOUT SPHINX & SUL BOOKS

Sphinx is the fiction imprint of Sul Books.

Born from a collaboration of two long-time independent esoteric publishers, and named to honor the Suleviae — the sisterhood of goddesses revered at springs throughout Europe — Sul Books is dedicated to publishing works that manifest aspects of the sacred sight that heals what humans have harmed.

As with the thrice-fold kinship of the Suleviae goddesses, Sul Books combines the publishing strength of three resilient imprints: Sphinx Books, RITONA, and Gods&Radicals Press. Arising from these continuing legacies comes a fourth imprint, Sul Books, committed to stand-out works of powerful transformation.

Each of our imprints is guided by a commitment to pluralism, dissent, and the autonomy of humans, with a core focus on the importance of indigenous, animist, and non-industrial ways of being in the world.

Find out more at Sulbooks.com

Like this book? Please leave a review for the author!